The Crock of Gold

The Crock of Gold

James Stephens

MINT EDITIONS

The Crock of Gold was first published in 1912.

This edition published by Mint Editions 2020.

ISBN 9781513266688 | E-ISBN 9781513267128

Published by Mint Editions®

 MINT
EDITIONS
minteditionbooks.com

Publishing Director: Jennifer Newens
Design & Production: Rachel Lopez Metzger
Typesetting: Westchester Publishing Services

Contents

BOOK 1
THE COMING OF PAN

Chapter 1

In the centre of the pine wood called Coilla Doraca there lived not long ago two Philosophers. They were wiser than anything else in the world except the Salmon who lies in the pool of Glyn Cagny into which the nuts of knowledge fall from the hazel bush on its bank. He, of course, is the most profound of living creatures, but the two Philosophers are next to him in wisdom. Their faces looked as though they were made of parchment, there was ink under their nails, and every difficulty that was submitted to them, even by women, they were able to instantly resolve. The Grey Woman of Dun Gortin and the Thin Woman of Inis Magrath asked them the three questions which nobody had ever been able to answer, and they were able to answer them. That was how they obtained the enmity of these two women which is more valuable than the friendship of angels. The Grey Woman and the Thin Woman were so incensed at being answered that they married the two Philosophers in order to be able to pinch them in bed, but the skins of the Philosophers were so thick that they did not know they were being pinched. They repaid the fury of the women with such tender affection that these vicious creatures almost expired of chagrin, and once, in a very ecstacy of exasperation, after having been kissed by their husbands, they uttered the fourteen hundred maledictions which comprised their wisdom, and these were learned by the Philosophers who thus became even wiser than before.

In due process of time two children were born of these marriages. They were born on the same day and in the same hour, and they were only different in this, that one of them was a boy and the other one was a girl. Nobody was able to tell how this had happened, and, for the first time in their lives, the Philosophers were forced to admire an event which they had been unable to prognosticate; but having proved by many different methods that the children were really children, that what must be must be, that a fact cannot be controverted, and that what has happened once may happen twice, they described the occurrence as extraordinary but not unnatural, and submitted peacefully to a Providence even wiser than they were.

The Philosopher who had the boy was very pleased because, he said, there were too many women in the world, and the Philosopher who had the girl was very pleased also because, he said, you cannot have too much of a good thing: the Grey Woman and the Thin Woman, however, were not in the least softened by maternity—they said that they had not bargained for it, that the children were gotten under false presences, that they were respectable married women, and that, as a protest against their wrongs, they would not cook any more food for the Philosophers. This was pleasant news for their husbands, who disliked the women's cooking very much, but they did not say so, for the women would certainly have insisted on their rights to cook had they imagined their husbands disliked the results: therefore, the Philosophers besought their wives every day to cook one of their lovely dinners again, and this the women always refused to do.

They all lived together in a small house in the very centre of a dark pine wood. Into this place the sun never shone because the shade was too deep, and no wind ever came there either, because the boughs were too thick, so that it was the most solitary and quiet place in the world, and the Philosophers were able to hear each other thinking all day long, or making speeches to each other, and these were the pleasantest sounds they knew of. To them there were only two kinds of sounds anywhere—these were conversation and noise: they liked the first very much indeed, but they spoke of the second with stern disapproval, and, even when it was made by a bird, a breeze, or a shower of rain, they grew angry and demanded that it should be abolished. Their wives seldom spoke at all and yet they were never silent: they communicated with each other by a kind of physical telegraphy which they had learned among the Shee—they cracked their finger-joints quickly or slowly and so were able to communicate with each other over immense distances, for by dint of long practice they could make great explosive sounds which were nearly like thunder, and gentler sounds like the tapping of grey ashes on a hearthstone. The Thin Woman hated her own child, but she loved the Grey Woman's baby, and the Grey Woman loved the Thin Woman's infant but could not abide her own. A compromise may put an end to the most perplexing of situations, and, consequently, the two women swapped children, and at once became the most tender and amiable mothers imaginable, and the families were able to live together in a more perfect amity than could be found anywhere else.

The children grew in grace and comeliness. At first the little boy was short and fat and the little girl was long and thin, then the little girl became round and chubby while the little boy grew lanky and wiry. This was because the little girl used to sit very quiet and be good and the little boy used not.

They lived for many years in the deep seclusion of the pine wood wherein a perpetual twilight reigned, and here they were wont to play their childish games, flitting among the shadowy trees like little quick shadows. At times their mothers, the Grey Woman and the Thin Woman, played with them, but this was seldom, and sometimes their fathers, the two Philosophers, came out and looked at them through spectacles which were very round and very glassy, and had immense circles of horn all round the edges. They had, however, other playmates with whom they could romp all day long. There were hundreds of rabbits running about in the brushwood; they were full of fun and were very fond of playing with the children. There were squirrels who joined cheerfully in their games, and some goats, having one day strayed in from the big world, were made so welcome that they always came again whenever they got the chance. There were birds also, crows and blackbirds and willy-wagtails, who were well acquainted with the youngsters, and visited them as frequently as their busy lives permitted.

At a short distance from their home there was a clearing in the wood about ten feet square; through this clearing, as through a funnel, the sun for a few hours in the summer time blazed down. It was the boy who first discovered the strange radiant shaft in the wood. One day he had been sent out to collect pine cones for the fire. As these were gathered daily the supply immediately near the house was scanty, therefore he had, while searching for more, wandered further from his home than usual. The first sight of the extraordinary blaze astonished him. He had never seen anything like it before, and the steady, unwinking glare aroused his fear and curiosity equally. Curiosity will conquer fear even more than bravery will; indeed, it has led many people into dangers which mere physical courage would shudder away from, for hunger and love and curiosity are the great impelling forces of life. When the little boy found that the light did not move he drew closer to it, and at last, emboldened by curiosity, he stepped right into it and found that it was not a thing at all. The instant that he stepped into the light he found it was hot, and this so frightened him that he jumped out of it again and ran behind a tree. Then he jumped into it for a moment and out of it again, and for nearly half an hour he played a splendid game of tip and tig with the sunlight. At last he grew quite bold and stood in it and found that it did not burn him at all, but he did not like to remain in it, fearing that he might be cooked. When he went home with the pine cones he said nothing to the Grey Woman of Dun Gortin or to the Thin Woman of Inis Magrath or to the two Philosophers, but he told the little girl all about it when they went to bed, and every day afterwards they used to go and play with the sunlight, and the rabbits and the squirrels would follow them there and join in their games with twice the interest they had shown before.

Chapter 2

To the lonely house in the pine wood people sometimes came for advice on subjects too recondite for even those extremes of elucidation, the parish priest and the tavern. These people were always well received, and their perplexities were attended to instantly, for the Philosophers liked being wise and they were not ashamed to put their learning to the proof, nor were they, as so many wise people are, fearful lest they should become poor or less respected by giving away their knowledge. These were favourite maxims with them:

You must be fit to give before you can be fit to receive.

Knowledge becomes lumber in a week, therefore, get rid of it.

The box must be emptied before it can be refilled.

Refilling is progress.

A sword, a spade, and a thought should never be allowed to rust.

The Grey Woman and the Thin Woman, however, held opinions quite contrary to these, and their maxims also were different:

A secret is a weapon and a friend.

Man is God's secret, Power is man's secret, Sex is woman's secret.

By having much you are fitted to have more.

There is always room in the box.

The art of packing is the last lecture of wisdom.

The scalp of your enemy is progress.

Holding these opposed views it seemed likely that visitors seeking for advice from the Philosophers might be astonished and captured by their wives; but the women were true to their own doctrines and refused to part with information to any persons saving only those of high rank, such as policemen, gombeen men, and district and county councillors; but even to these they charged high prices for their information, and a bonus on any gains which accrued through the following of their advices. It is unnecessary to state that their following was small when compared with those who sought the assistance of their husbands, for scarcely a week passed but some person came through the pine wood with his brows in a tangle of perplexity.

In these people the children were deeply interested. They used to go apart afterwards and talk about them, and would try to remember what they looked like, how they talked, and their manner of walking or taking snuff. After a time they became interested in the problems which these people submitted to their parents and the replies or instructions wherewith the latter relieved them. Long training had made the children able to sit perfectly quiet, so that when the talk came to the interesting part they were entirely forgotten, and ideas which might otherwise have been spared their youth became the commonplaces of their conversation.

When the children were ten years of age one of the Philosophers died. He called the household together and announced that the time had come when he must bid them all good-bye, and that his intention was to die as quickly as might be. It was, he continued, an unfortunate thing that his health was at the moment more robust than it had been for a long time, but that, of course, was no obstacle to his resolution, for death did not depend upon ill-health but upon a multitude of other factors with the details whereof he would not trouble them.

His wife, the Grey Woman of Dun Gortin, applauded this resolution and added as an amendment that it was high time he did something, that the life he had been leading was an arid and unprofitable one, that he had stolen her fourteen hundred maledictions for which he had no use and presented her with a child for which she had none, and that, all things concerned, the sooner he did die and stop talking the sooner everybody concerned would be made happy.

The other Philosopher replied mildly as he lit his pipe: "Brother, the greatest of all virtues is curiosity, and the end of all desire is wisdom; tell us, therefore, by what steps you have arrived at this commendable resolution."

To this the Philosopher replied: "I have attained to all the wisdom which I am fitted to bear. In the space of one week no new truth has come to me. All that I have read lately I knew before; all that I have thought has been but a recapitulation of old and wearisome ideas. There is no longer an horizon before my eyes. Space has narrowed to the petty dimensions of my thumb. Time is the tick of a clock. Good and evil are two peas in the one pod. My wife's face is the same for ever. I want to play with the children, and yet I do not want to. Your conversation with me, brother, is like the droning of a bee in a dark cell. The pine trees take root and grow and die.—It's all bosh. Good-bye."

His friend replied:

"Brother, these are weighty reflections, and I do clearly perceive that the time has come for you to stop. I might observe, not in order to combat your views, but merely to continue an interesting conversation, that there are still some knowledges which you have not assimilated—

you do not yet know how to play the tambourine, nor how to be nice to your wife, nor how to get up first in the morning and cook the breakfast. Have you learned how to smoke strong tobacco as I do? or can you dance in the moonlight with a woman of the Shee? To understand the theory which underlies all things is not sufficient. It has occurred to me, brother, that wisdom may not be the end of everything. Goodness and kindliness are, perhaps, beyond wisdom. Is it not possible that the ultimate end is gaiety and music and a dance of joy? Wisdom is the oldest of all things. Wisdom is all head and no heart. Behold, brother, you are being crushed under the weight of your head. You are dying of old age while you are yet a child."

"Brother," replied the other Philosopher, "your voice is like the droning of a bee in a dark cell. If in my latter days I am reduced to playing on the tambourine and running after a hag in the moonlight, and cooking your breakfast in the grey morning, then it is indeed time that I should die. Good-bye, brother."

So saying, the Philosopher arose and removed all the furniture to the sides of the room so that there was a clear space left in the centre. He then took off his boots and his coat, and standing on his toes he commenced to gyrate with extraordinary rapidity. In a few moments his movements became steady and swift, and a sound came from him like the humming of a swift saw; this sound grew deeper and deeper, and at last continuous, so that the room was filled with a thrilling noise. In a quarter of an hour the movement began to noticeably slacken. In another three minutes it was quite slow. In two more minutes he grew visible again as a body, and then he wobbled to and fro, and at last dropped in a heap on the floor. He was quite dead, and on his face was an expression of serene beatitude.

"God be with you, brother," said the remaining Philosopher, and he lit his pipe, focused his vision on the extreme tip of his nose, and began to meditate profoundly on the aphorism whether the good is the all or the all is the good. In another moment he would have become oblivious of the room, the company, and the corpse, but the Grey Woman of Dun Gortin shattered his meditation by a demand for advice as to what should next be done. The Philosopher, with an effort, detached his eyes from his nose and his mind from his maxim.

"Chaos," said he, "is the first condition. Order is the first law. Continuity is the first reflection. Quietude is the first happiness. Our brother is dead—bury him." So saying, he returned his eyes to his nose, and his mind to his maxim, and lapsed to a profound reflection wherein nothing sat perched on insubstantiality, and the Spirit of Artifice goggled at the puzzle.

The Grey Woman of Dun Gortin took a pinch of snuff from her box and raised the keen over her husband:

"You were my husband and you are dead.

It is wisdom that has killed you.

If you had listened to my wisdom instead of to your own you would still be a trouble to me and I would still be happy.

Women are stronger than men—they do not die of wisdom.

They are better than men because they do not seek wisdom.

They are wiser than men because they know less and understand more.

I had fourteen hundred maledictions, my little store, and by a trick you stole them and left me empty.

You stole my wisdom and it has broken your neck.

I lost my knowledge and I am yet alive raising the keen over your body, but it was too heavy for you, my little knowledge.

You will never go out into the pine wood in the morning, or wander abroad on a night of stars.

You will not sit in the chimney-corner on the hard nights, or go to bed, or rise again, or do anything at all from this day out.

Who will gather pine cones now when the fire is going down, or call my name in the empty house, or be angry when the kettle is not boiling?

Now I am desolate indeed. I have no knowledge, I have no husband, I have no more to say."

"If I had anything better you should have it," said she politely to the Thin Woman of Inis Magrath.

"Thank you," said the Thin Woman, "it was very nice. Shall I begin now? My husband is meditating and we may be able to annoy him."

"Don't trouble yourself," replied the other, "I am past enjoyment and am, moreover, a respectable woman."

"That is no more than the truth, indeed."

"I have always done the right thing at the right time."

"I'd be the last body in the world to deny that," was the warm response.

"Very well, then," said the Grey Woman, and she commenced to take off her boots. She stood in the centre of the room and balanced herself on her toe.

"You are a decent, respectable lady," said the Thin Woman of Inis Magrath, and then the Grey Woman began to gyrate rapidly and more rapidly until she was a very fervour of motion, and in three-quarters of an hour (for she was very tough) she began to slacken, grew visible, wobbled, and fell beside her dead husband, and on her face was a beatitude almost surpassing his.

The Thin Woman of Inis Magrath smacked the children and put them to bed, next she buried the two bodies under the hearthstone, and then, with some trouble, detached her husband from his meditations. When he became capable of ordinary occurrences she detailed all that had happened, and said that he alone was to blame for the sad bereavement. He replied:

"The toxin generates the anti-toxin. The end lies concealed in the beginning. All bodies grow around a skeleton. Life is a petticoat about death. I will not go to bed."

Chapter 3

On the day following this melancholy occurrence Meehawl MacMurrachu, a small farmer in the neighbourhood, came through the pine trees with tangled brows. At the door of the little house he said, "God be with all here," and marched in.

The Philosopher removed his pipe from his lips—

"God be with yourself," said he, and he replaced his pipe.

Meehawl MacMurrachu crooked his thumb at space, "Where is the other one?" said he.

"Ah!" said the Philosopher.

"He might be outside, maybe?"

"He might, indeed," said the Philosopher gravely.

"Well, it doesn't matter," said the visitor, "for you have enough knowledge by yourself to stock a shop. The reason I came here to-day was to ask your honoured advice about my wife's washing-board. She only has it a couple of years, and the last time she used it was when she washed out my Sunday shirt and her black skirt with the red things on it—you know the one?"

"I do not," said the Philosopher.

"Well, anyhow, the washboard is gone, and my wife says it was either taken by the fairies or by Bessie Hannigan—you know Bessie Hannigan? She has whiskers like a goat and a lame leg!" "I do not," said the Philosopher.

"No matter," said Meehawl MacMurrachu. "She didn't take it, because my wife got her out yesterday and kept her talking for two hours while I went through everything in her bit of a house—the washboard wasn't there."

"It wouldn't be," said the Philosopher.

"Maybe your honour could tell a body where it is then?"

"Maybe I could," said the Philosopher; "are you listening?"

"I am," said Meehawl MacMurrachu.

The Philosopher drew his chair closer to the visitor until their knees were jammed together. He laid both his hands on Meehawl MacMurrachu's knees "Washing is an extraordinary custom," said he. "We are washed both on coming into the world and on going out of it, and we take no pleasure from the first washing nor any profit from the last."

"True for you, sir," said Meehawl MacMurrachu.

"Many people consider that scourings supplementary to these are only due to habit. Now, habit is continuity of action, it is a most detestable thing and is very difficult to get away from. A proverb will run where a writ will not, and the follies of our forefathers are of greater importance to us than is the well-being of our posterity."

"I wouldn't say a word against that, sir," said Meehawl MacMurrachu.

"Cats are a philosophic and thoughtful race, but they do not admit the efficacy of either water or soap, and yet it is usually conceded that they are cleanly folk. There are exceptions to every rule, and I once knew a cat who lusted after water and bathed daily: he was an unnatural brute and died ultimately of the head staggers. Children are nearly as wise as cats. It is true that they will utilize water in a variety of ways, for instance, the destruction of a tablecloth or a pinafore, and I have observed them greasing a ladder with soap, showing in the process a great knowledge of the properties of this material."

"Why shouldn't they, to be sure?" said Meehawl MacMurrachu. "Have you got a match, sir?"

"I have not," said the Philosopher. "Sparrows, again, are a highly acute and reasonable folk. They use water to quench thirst, but when they are dirty they take a dust bath and are at once cleansed. Of course, birds are often seen in the water, but they go there to catch fish and not to wash. I have often fancied that fish are a dirty, sly, and unintelligent people—this is due to their staying so much in the water, and it has been observed that on being removed from this element they at once expire through sheer ecstasy at escaping from their prolonged washing."

"I have seen them doing it myself," said Meehawl. "Did you ever hear, sir, about the fish that Paudeen MacLoughlin caught in the policeman's hat."

"I did not," said the Philosopher. "The first person who washed was possibly a person seeking a cheap notoriety. Any fool can wash himself, but every wise man knows that it is an unnecessary labour, for nature will quickly reduce him to a natural and healthy dirtiness again. We should seek, therefore, not how to make ourselves clean, but how to attain a more unique and splendid dirtiness, and perhaps the accumulated layers of matter might, by ordinary geologic compulsion, become incorporated with the human cuticle and so render clothing unnecessary—"

"About that washboard," said Meehawl, "I was just going to say—"

"It doesn't matter," said the Philosopher. "In its proper place I admit the necessity for water. As a thing to sail a ship on it can scarcely be surpassed (not, you will understand, that I entirely approve of ships, they tend to create and perpetuate international curiosity and the smaller vermin of different latitudes). As an element wherewith to put out a fire, or brew tea, or make a slide in winter it is useful, but in a tin basin it has a repulsive and meagre aspect.—Now as to your wife's washboard—"

"Good luck to your honour," said Meehawl.

"Your wife says that either the fairies or a woman with a goat's leg has it."

"It's her whiskers," said Meehawl.

"They are lame," said the Philosopher sternly.

"Have it your own way, sir, I'm not certain now how the creature is afflicted."

"You say that this unhealthy woman has not got your wife's washboard. It remains, therefore, that the fairies have it."

"It looks that way," said Meehawl.

"There are six clans of fairies living in this neighbourhood; but the process of elimination, which has shaped the world to a globe, the ant to its environment, and man to the captaincy of the vertebrates, will not fail in this instance either."

"Did you ever see anything like the way wasps have increased this season?" said Meehawl; "faith, you can't sit down anywhere but your breeches—"

"I did not," said the Philosopher. "Did you leave out a pan of milk on last Tuesday?"

"I did then."

"Do you take off your hat when you meet a dust twirl?"

"I wouldn't neglect that," said Meehawl.

"Did you cut down a thorn bush recently?"

"I'd sooner cut my eye out," said Meehawl, "and go about as wall-eyed as Lorcan O'Nualain's ass: I would that. Did you ever see his ass, sir? It—"

"I did not," said the Philosopher. "Did you kill a robin redbreast?"

"Never," said Meehawl. "By the pipers," he added, "that old skinny cat of mine caught a bird on the roof yesterday."

"Hah!" cried the Philosopher, moving, if it were possible, even closer to his client, "now we have it. It is the Leprecauns of Gort na Cloca

Mora took your washboard. Go to the Gort at once. There is a hole under a tree in the south-east of the field. Try what you will find in that hole."

"I'll do that," said Meehawl. "Did you ever—"

"I did not," said the Philosopher.

So Meehawl MacMurrachu went away and did as he had been bidden, and underneath the tree of Gort na Cloca Mora he found a little crock of gold.

"There's a power of washboards in that," said he.

By reason of this incident the fame of the Philosopher became even greater than it had been before, and also by reason of it many singular events were to happen with which you shall duly become acquainted.

Chapter 4

It so happened that the Leprecauns of Gort na Cloca Mora were not thankful to the Philosopher for having sent Meehawl MacMurrachu to their field. In stealing Meehawl's property they were quite within their rights because their bird had undoubtedly been slain by his cat. Not alone, therefore, was their righteous vengeance nullified, but the crock of gold which had taken their community many thousands of years to amass was stolen. A Leprecaun without a pot of gold is like a rose without perfume, a bird without a wing, or an inside without an outside. They considered that the Philosopher had treated them badly, that his action was mischievous and unneighbourly, and that until they were adequately compensated for their loss both of treasure and dignity, no conditions other than those of enmity could exist between their people and the little house in the pine wood. Furthermore, for them the situation was cruelly complicated. They were unable to organise a direct, personal hostility against their new enemy, because the Thin Woman of Inis Magrath would certainly protect her husband. She belonged to the Shee of Croghan Conghaile, who had relatives in every fairy fort in Ireland, and were also strongly represented in the forts and duns of their immediate neighbours. They could, of course, have called an extraordinary meeting of the Sheogs, Leprecauns, and Cluricauns, and presented their case with a claim for damages against the Shee of Croghan Conghaile, but that Clann would assuredly repudiate any liability on the ground that no member of their fraternity was responsible for the outrage, as it was the Philosopher, and not the Thin Woman of Inis Magrath, who had done the deed. Notwithstanding this they were unwilling to let the matter rest, and the fact that justice was out of reach only added fury to their anger.

One of their number was sent to interview the Thin Woman of Inis Magrath, and the others concentrated nightly about the dwelling of Meehawl MacMurrachu in an endeavour to recapture the treasure which they were quite satisfied was hopeless. They found that Meehawl, who understood the customs of the Earth Folk very well, had buried the crock of gold beneath a thorn bush, thereby placing it under the protection of every fairy in the world—the Leprecauns themselves included, and until it was removed from this place by human hands they were bound to respect its hiding-place, and even guarantee its safety with their blood.

They afflicted Meehawl with an extraordinary attack of rheumatism and his wife with an equally virulent sciatica, but they got no lasting pleasure from their groans.

The Leprecaun, who had been detailed to visit the Thin Woman of Inis Magrath, duly arrived at the cottage in the pine wood and made his complaint. The little man wept as he told the story, and the two children wept out of sympathy for him. The Thin Woman said she was desperately grieved by the whole unpleasant transaction, and that all her sympathies were with Gort na Cloca Mora, but that she must disassociate herself from any responsibility in the matter as it was her husband who was the culpable person, and that she had no control over his mental processes, which, she concluded, was one of the seven curious things in the world.

As her husband was away in a distant part of the wood nothing further could be done at that time, so the Leprecaun returned again to his fellows without any good news, but he promised to come back early on the following day. When the Philosopher come home late that night the Thin Woman was waiting up for him.

"Woman," said the Philosopher, "you ought to be in bed."

"Ought I indeed?" said the Thin Woman. "I'd have you know that I'll go to bed when I like and get up when I like without asking your or any one else's permission."

"That is not true," said the Philosopher. "You get sleepy whether you like it or not, and you awaken again without your permission being asked. Like many other customs such as singing, dancing, music, and acting, sleep has crept into popular favour as part of a religious ceremonial. Nowhere can one go to sleep more easily than in a church."

"Do you know," said the Thin Woman, "that a Leprecaun came here to-day?"

"I do not," said the Philosopher, "and notwithstanding the innumerable centuries which have elapsed since that first sleeper (probably with extreme difficulty) sank into his religious trance, we can to-day sleep through a religious ceremony with an ease which would have been a source of wealth and fame to that prehistoric worshipper and his acolytes."

"Are you going to listen to what I am telling you about the Leprecaun?" said the Thin Woman.

"I am not," said the Philosopher. "It has been suggested that we go to sleep at night because it is then too dark to do anything else; but owls, who are a venerably sagacious folk, do not sleep in the night time. Bats, also, are a very clear-minded race; they sleep in the broadest day, and they do it in a charming manner. They clutch the branch of a tree with their toes and hang head downwards—a position which I consider singularly happy, for the rush of blood to the head consequent on this inverted position should engender a drowsiness and a certain imbecility of mind which must either sleep or explode."

"Will you never be done talking?" shouted the Thin Woman passionately.

"I will not," said the Philosopher. "In certain ways sleep is useful. It is an excellent way of listening to an opera or seeing pictures on a bioscope. As a medium for day-dreams I know of nothing that can equal it. As an accomplishment it is graceful, but as a means of spending a night it is intolerably ridiculous. If you were going to say anything, my love, please say it now, but you should always remember to think before you speak. A woman should be seen seldom but never heard. Quietness is the beginning of virtue. To be silent is to be beautiful. Stars do not make a noise. Children should always be in bed. These are serious truths, which cannot be controverted; therefore, silence is fitting as regards them."

"Your stirabout is on the hob," said the Thin Woman. "You can get it for yourself. I would not move the breadth of my nail if you were dying of hunger. I hope there's lumps in it. A Leprecaun from Gort na Cloca Mora was here to-day. They'll give it to you for robbing their pot of gold. You old thief, you! you lobeared, crock-kneed fat-eye!"

The Thin Woman whizzed suddenly from where she stood and leaped into bed. From beneath the blanket she turned a vivid, furious eye on her husband. She was trying to give him rheumatism and toothache and lockjaw all at once. If she had been satisfied to concentrate her attention on one only of these torments she might have succeeded in afflicting her husband according to her wish, but she was not able to do that.

"Finality is death. Perfection is finality. Nothing is perfect. There are lumps in it," said the Philosopher.

Chapter 5

When the Leprecaun came through the pine wood on the following day he met two children at a little distance from the house. He raised his open right hand above his head (this is both the fairy and the Gaelic form of salutation), and would have passed on but that a thought brought him to a halt. Sitting down before the two children he stared at them for a long time, and they stared back at him. At last he said to the boy:

"What is your name, a vic vig O?"

"Seumas Beg, sir," the boy replied.

"It's a little name," said the Leprecaun.

"It's what my mother calls me, sir," returned the boy.

"What does your father call you," was the next question.

"Seumas Roghan Maelduin O'Carbhail Mac an Droid."

"It's a big name," said the Leprecaun, and he turned to the little girl. "What is your name, a cailin vig O?"

"Brigid Beg, sir."

"And what does your father call you?"

"He never calls me at all, sir."

"Well, Seumaseen and Breedeen, you are good little children, and I like you very much. Health be with you until I come to see you again."

And then the Leprecaun went back the way he had come. As he went he made little jumps and cracked his fingers, and sometimes he rubbed one leg against the other.

"That's a nice Leprecaun," said Seumas.

"I like him too," said Brigid.

"Listen," said Seumas, "let me be the Leprecaun, and you be the two children, and I will ask you our names."

So they did that.

The next day the Leprecaun came again. He sat down beside the children and, as before, he was silent for a little time.

"Are you not going to ask us our names, sir?" said Seumas.

His sister smoothed out her dress shyly. "My name, sir, is Brigid Beg," said she.

"Did you ever play Jackstones?" said the Leprecaun.

"No, sir," replied Seumas.

"I'll teach you how to play Jackstones," said the Leprecaun, and he picked up some pine cones and taught the children that game.

"Did you ever play Ball in the Decker?"

"No, sir," said Seumas.

"Did you ever play 'I can make a nail with my ree-roraddy-O, I can make a nail with my ree-ro-ray'?"

"No, sir," replied Seumas.

"It's a nice game," said the Leprecaun, "and so is Capon-the-back, and Twenty-four yards on the Billy-goat's Tail, and Towns, and Relievo, and Leap-frog. I'll teach you all these games," said the Leprecaun, "and I'll teach you how to play Knifey, and Hole-and-taw, and Horneys and Robbers.

"Leap-frog is the best one to start with, so I'll teach it to you at once. Let you bend down like this, Breedeen, and you bend down like that a good distance away, Seumas. Now I jump over Breedeen's back, and then I run and jump over Seumaseen's back like this, and then I run ahead again and I bend down. Now, Breedeen, you jump over your brother, and then you jump over me, and run a good bit on and bend down again. Now, Seumas, it's your turn; you jump over me and then over your sister, and then you run on and bend down again and I jump."

"This is a fine game, sir," said Seumas.

"It is, a vic vig,—keep in your head," said the Leprecaun. "That's a good jump, you couldn't beat that jump, Seumas."

"I can jump better than Brigid already," replied Seumas, "and I'll jump as well as you do when I get more practice—keep in your head, sir."

Almost without noticing it they had passed through the edge of the wood, and were playing into a rough field which was cumbered with big, grey rocks. It was the very last field in sight, and behind it the rough, heather-packed mountain sloped distantly away to the skyline. There was a raggedy blackberry hedge all round the field, and there were long, tough, haggard-looking plants growing in clumps here and there. Near a corner of this field there was a broad, low tree, and as they played they came near and nearer to it. The Leprecaun gave a back very close to the tree. Seumas ran and jumped and slid down a hole at the side of the tree. Then Brigid ran and jumped and slid down the same hole.

"Dear me!" said Brigid, and she flashed out of sight.

The Leprecaun cracked his fingers and rubbed one leg against the other, and then he also dived into the hole and disappeared from view.

When the time at which the children usually went home had passed, the Thin Woman of Inis Magrath became a little anxious. She had never known them to be late for dinner before. There was one of the children whom she hated; it was her own child, but as she had forgotten which of them was hers, and as she loved one of them, she was compelled to love both for fear of making a mistake and chastising the child for whom her heart secretly yearned. Therefore, she was equally concerned about both of them.

Dinner time passed and supper time arrived, but the children did not. Again and again the Thin Woman went out through the dark pine trees and called until she was so hoarse that she could not even hear herself when she roared. The evening wore on to the night, and while she waited for the Philosopher to come in she reviewed the situation. Her husband had not come in, the children had not come in, the Leprecaun had not returned as arranged. . . A light flashed upon her. The Leprecaun had kidnapped her children! She announced a vengeance against the Leprecauns which would stagger humanity. While in the extreme centre of her ecstasy the Philosopher came through the trees and entered the house.

The Thin Woman flew to him—

"Husband," said she, "the Leprecauns of Gort na Cloca Mora have kidnapped our children."

The Philosopher gazed at her for a moment.

"Kidnapping," said he, "has been for many centuries a favourite occupation of fairies, gypsies, and the brigands of the East. The usual procedure is to attach a person and hold it to ransom. If the ransom is not paid an ear or a finger may be cut from the captive and despatched to those interested, with the statement that an arm or a leg will follow in a week unless suitable arrangements are entered into."

"Do you understand," said the Thin Woman passionately, "that it is your own children who have been kidnapped?"

"I do not," said the Philosopher. "This course, however, is rarely followed by the fairy people: they do not ordinarily steal for ransom, but for love of thieving, or from some other obscure and possibly functional causes, and the victim is retained in their forts or duns until by the effluxion of time they forget their origin and become peaceable citizens of the fairy state. Kidnapping is not by any means confined to either humanity or the fairy people."

"Monster," said the Thin Woman in a deep voice, "will you listen to me?"

"I will not," said the Philosopher. "Many of the insectivora also practice this custom. Ants, for example, are a respectable race living in well-ordered communities. They have attained to a most complex and artificial civilization, and will frequently adventure far afield on colonising or other expeditions from whence they return with a rich booty of aphides and other stock, who thenceforward become the servants and domestic creatures of the republic. As they neither kill nor eat their captives, this practice will be termed kidnapping. The same may be said of bees, a hardy and industrious race living in hexagonal cells which are very difficult to make. Sometimes, on lacking a queen of their own, they have been observed to abduct one from a less powerful neighbour, and use her for their own purposes without shame, mercy, or remorse."

"Will you not understand?" screamed the Thin Woman.

"I will not," said the Philosopher. "Semi-tropical apes have been rumoured to kidnap children, and are reported to use them very tenderly indeed, sharing their coconuts, yams, plantains, and other equatorial provender with the largest generosity, and conveying their delicate captives from tree to tree (often at great distances from each other and from the ground) with the most guarded solicitude and benevolence."

"I am going to bed," said the Thin Woman, "your stirabout is on the hob."

"Are there lumps in it, my dear?" said the Philosopher.

"I hope there are," replied the Thin Woman, and she leaped into bed.

That night the Philosopher was afflicted with the most extraordinary attack of rheumatism he had ever known, nor did he get any ease until the grey morning wearied his lady into a reluctant slumber.

Chapter 6

The Thin Woman of Inis Magrath slept very late that morning, but when she did awaken her impatience was so urgent that she could scarcely delay to eat her breakfast. Immediately after she had eaten she put on her bonnet and shawl and went through the pine wood in the direction of Gort na Cloca Mora. In a short time she reached the rocky field, and, walking over to the tree in the southeast corner, she picked up a small stone and hammered loudly against the trunk of the tree. She hammered in a peculiar fashion, giving two knocks and then three knocks, and then one knock. A voice came up from the hole.

"Who is that, please?" said the voice.

"Ban na Droid of Inis Magrath, and well you know it," was her reply.

"I am coming up, Noble Woman," said the voice, and in another moment the Leprecaun leaped out of the hole.

"Where are Seumas and Brigid Beg?" said the Thin Woman sternly.

"How would I know where they are?" replied the Leprecaun. "Wouldn't they be at home now?"

"If they were at home I wouldn't have come here looking for them," was her reply. "It is my belief that you have them."

"Search me," said the Leprecaun, opening his waistcoat.

"They are down there in your little house," said the Thin Woman angrily, "and the sooner you let them up the better it will be for yourself and your five brothers."

"Noble Woman," said the Leprecaun, "you can go down yourself into our little house and look. I can't say fairer than that."

"I wouldn't fit down there," said she. "I'm too big."

"You know the way for making yourself little," replied the Leprecaun.

"But I mightn't be able to make myself big again," said the Thin Woman, "and then you and your dirty brothers would have it all your own way. If you don't let the children up," she continued, "I'll raise the Shee of Croghan Conghaile against you. You know what happened to the Cluricauns of Oilean na Glas when they stole the Queen's baby—It will be a worse thing than that for you. If the children are not back in my house before moonrise this night, I'll go round to my people. Just tell that to your five ugly brothers. Health with you," she added, and strode away.

"Health with yourself, Noble Woman," said the Leprecaun, and he stood on one leg until she was out of sight and then he slid down into the hole again.

When the Thin Woman was going back through the pine wood she saw Meehawl MacMurrachu travelling in the same direction and his brows were in a tangle of perplexity.

"God be with you, Meehawl MacMurrachu," said she.

"God and Mary be with you, ma'am," he replied, "I am in great trouble this day."

"Why wouldn't you be?" said the Thin Woman.

"I came up to have a talk with your husband about a particular thing."

"If it's talk you want you have come to a good house, Meehawl."

"He's a powerful man right enough," said Meehawl.

After a few minutes the Thin Woman spoke again. "I can get the reek of his pipe from here. Let you go right in to him now and I'll stay outside for a while, for the sound of your two voices would give me a pain in my head."

"Whatever will please you will please me, ma'am," said her companion, and he went into the little house.

Meehawl MacMurrachu had good reason to be perplexed. He was the father of one child only, and she was the most beautiful girl in the whole world. The pity of it was that no one at all knew she was beautiful, and she did not even know it herself. At times when she bathed in the eddy of a mountain stream and saw her reflection looking up from the placid water she thought that she looked very nice, and then a great sadness would come upon her, for what is the use of looking nice if there is nobody to see one's beauty? Beauty, also, is usefulness. The arts as well as the crafts, the graces equally with the utilities must stand up in the marketplace and be judged by the gombeen men.

The only house near to her father's was that occupied by Bessie Hannigan. The other few houses were scattered widely with long, quiet miles of hill and bog between them, so that she had hardly seen more than a couple of men beside her father since she was born. She helped her father and mother in all the small businesses of their house, and every day also she drove their three cows and two goats to pasture on the mountain slopes. Here through the sunny days the years had passed in a slow, warm thoughtlessness wherein, without thinking, many thoughts had entered into her mind and many pictures hung for a moment like birds in the thin air. At first, and for a long time, she had been happy enough; there were many things in which a child might be interested: the spacious heavens which never wore the same beauty on any day; the innumerable little creatures living among the grasses or in the heather; the steep swing of a bird down from the mountain to the infinite plains below; the little flowers which were so contented each in its peaceful place; the bees gathering food for their houses, and the stout beetles who are always losing their way in the dusk. These things, and many others, interested her. The three cows after they had grazed for a long time would come and lie by her side and look at her as they chewed their cud, and the goats would prance from the bracken to push their heads against her breast because they loved her.

Indeed, everything in her quiet world loved this girl: but very slowly there was growing in her consciousness an unrest, a disquietude to which she had hitherto been a stranger. Sometimes an infinite weariness oppressed her to the earth. A thought was born in her mind and it had no name. It was growing and could not be expressed. She had no words wherewith to meet it, to exorcise or greet this stranger who, more and more insistently and pleadingly, tapped upon her doors and begged to be spoken to, admitted and caressed and nourished. A thought is a real thing and words are only its raiment, but a thought is as shy as a virgin; unless it is fittingly apparelled we may not look on its shadowy nakedness: it will fly from us and only return again in the darkness crying in a thin, childish voice which we may not comprehend until, with aching minds, listening and divining, we at last fashion for it those symbols which are its protection and its banner. So she could not understand the touch that came to her from afar and yet how intimately, the whisper so aloof and yet so thrillingly personal. The standard of either language or experience was not hers; she could listen but not think, she could feel but not know, her eyes looked forward and did not see, her hands groped in the sunlight and felt nothing. It was like the edge of a little wind which stirred her tresses but could not lift them, or the first white peep of the dawn which is neither light nor darkness. But she listened, not with her ears but with her blood. The fingers of her soul stretched out to clasp a stranger's hand, and her disquietude was quickened through with an eagerness which was neither physical nor mental, for neither her body nor her mind was definitely interested. Some dim region between these grew alarmed and watched and waited and did not sleep or grow weary at all.

One morning she lay among the long, warm grasses. She watched a bird who soared and sang for a little time, and then it sped swiftly away down the steep air and out of sight in the blue distance. Even when it was gone the song seemed to ring in her ears. It seemed to linger with her as a faint, sweet echo, coming fitfully, with little pauses as though a wind disturbed it, and careless, distant eddies. After a few moments she knew it was not a bird. No bird's song had that consecutive melody, for their themes are as careless as their wings. She sat up and looked about her, but there was nothing in sight: the mountains sloped gently above her and away to the clear sky; around her the scattered clumps of heather were drowsing in the sunlight; far below she could see her father's house, a little grey patch near some trees—and then the music stopped and left her wondering.

She could not find her goats anywhere although for a long time she searched. They came to her at last of their own accord from behind a fold in the hills, and they were more wildly excited than she had ever seen them before. Even the cows forsook their solemnity and broke into awkward gambols around her. As she walked home that evening a strange elation taught her feet to dance. Hither and thither she flitted in front of the beasts and behind them. Her feet tripped to a wayward measure. There was a tune in her ears and she danced to it, throwing her arms out and above her head and swaying and bending as she went. The full freedom of her body was hers now: the lightness and poise and certainty of her limbs delighted her, and the strength that did not tire delighted her also. The evening was full of peace and quietude, the mellow, dusky sunlight made a path for her feet, and everywhere through the wide fields birds were flashing and singing, and she sang with them a song that had no words and wanted none.

The following day she heard the music again, faint and thin, wonderfully sweet and as wild as the song of a bird, but it was a melody which no bird would adhere to. A theme was repeated again and again. In the middle of trills, grace-notes, runs and catches it recurred with a strange, almost holy, solemnity,—a hushing, slender melody full of austerity and aloofness. There was something in it to set her heart beating. She yearned to it with her ears and her lips. Was it joy, menace, carelessness? She did not know, but this she did know, that however terrible it was personal to her. It was her unborn thought strangely audible and felt rather than understood.

On that day she did not see anybody either. She drove her charges home in the evening listlessly and the beasts also were very quiet.

When the music came again she made no effort to discover where it came from. She only listened, and when the tune was ended she saw a figure rise from the fold of a little hill. The sunlight was gleaming from his arms and shoulders but the rest of his body was hidden by the bracken, and he did not look at her as he went away playing softly on a double pipe.

The next day he did look at her. He stood waist-deep in greenery fronting her squarely. She had never seen so strange a face before. Her eyes almost died on him as she gazed and he returned her look for a long minute with an intent, expressionless regard. His hair was a cluster of brown curls, his nose was little and straight, and his wide mouth drooped sadly at the corners. His eyes were wide and most mournful, and his forehead was very broad and white. His sad eyes and mouth almost made her weep.

When he turned away he smiled at her, and it was as though the sun had shone suddenly in a dark place, banishing all sadness and gloom. Then he went mincingly away. As he went he lifted the slender double reed to his lips and blew a few careless notes.

The next day he fronted her as before, looking down to her eyes from a short distance. He played for only a few moments, and fitfully, and then he came to her. When he left the bracken the girl suddenly clapped her hands against her eyes affrighted. There was something different, terrible about him. The upper part of his body was beautiful, but the lower part. . . She dared not look at him again. She would have risen and fled away but she feared he might pursue her, and the thought of such a chase and the inevitable capture froze her blood. The thought of anything behind us is always terrible. The sound of pursuing feet is worse than the murder from which we fly—So she sat still and waited but nothing happened. At last, desperately, she dropped her hands. He was sitting on the ground a few paces from her. He was not looking at her but far away sidewards across the spreading hill. His legs were crossed; they were shaggy and hoofed like the legs of a goat: but she would not look at these because of his wonderful, sad, grotesque face. Gaiety is good to look upon and an innocent face is delightful to our souls, but no woman can resist sadness or weakness, and ugliness she dare not resist. Her nature leaps to be the comforter. It is her reason. It exalts her to an ecstasy wherein nothing but the sacrifice of herself has any proportion. Men are not fathers by instinct but by chance, but women are mothers beyond thought, beyond instinct which is the father of thought. Motherliness, pity, self-sacrifice—these are the charges of her primal cell, and not even the discovery that men are comedians, liars, and egotists will wean her from this. As she looked at the pathos of his face she repudiated the hideousness of his body. The beast which is in all men is glossed by women; it is his childishness, the destructive energy inseparable from youth and high spirits, and it is always forgiven by women, often forgotten, sometimes, and not rarely, cherished and fostered.

After a few moments of this silence he placed the reed to his lips and played a plaintive little air, and then he spoke to her in a strange voice, coming like a wind from distant places.

"What is your name, Shepherd Girl?" said he.

"Caitilin, Ingin Ni Murrachu," she whispered.

"Daughter of Murrachu," said he, "I have come from a far place where there are high hills. The men and maidens who follow their flocks in that place know me and love me for I am the Master of the Shepherds. They sing and dance and are glad when I come to them in the sunlight; but in this country no people have done any reverence to me. The shepherds fly away when they hear my pipes in the pastures; the maidens scream in fear when I dance to them in the meadows. I am very lonely in this strange country. You also, although you danced to the music of my pipes, have covered your face against me and made no reverence."

"I will do whatever you say if it is right," said she.

"You must not do anything because it is right, but because it is your wish. Right is a word and Wrong is a word, but the sun shines in the morning and the dew falls in the dusk without thinking of these words which have no meaning. The bee flies to the flower and the seed goes abroad and is happy. Is that right, Shepherd Girl?—it is wrong also. I come to you because the bee goes to the flower—it is wrong! If I did not come to you to whom would I go? There is no right and no wrong but only the will of the gods."

"I am afraid of you," said the girl.

"You fear me because my legs are shaggy like the legs of a goat. Look at them well, O Maiden, and know that they are indeed the legs of a beast and then you will not be afraid any more. Do you not love beasts? Surely you should love them for they yearn to you humbly or fiercely, craving your hand upon their heads as I do. If I were not fashioned thus I would not come to you because I would not need you. Man is a god and a brute. He aspires to the stars with his head but his feet are contented in the grasses of the field, and when he forsakes the brute upon which he stands then there will be no more men and no more women and the immortal gods will blow this world away like smoke."

"I don't know what you want me to do," said the girl.

"I want you to want me. I want you to forget right and wrong; to be as happy as the beasts, as careless as the flowers and the birds. To live to the depths of your nature as well as to the heights. Truly there are stars in the heights and they will be a garland for your forehead. But the depths are equal to the heights. Wondrous deep are the depths, very fertile is the lowest deep. There are stars there also, brighter than the stars on high. The name of the heights is Wisdom and the name of the depths is Love. How shall they come together and be fruitful if you do not plunge deeply and fearlessly? Wisdom is the spirit and the wings of the spirit, Love is the shaggy beast that goes down. Gallantly he dives, below thought, beyond Wisdom, to rise again as high above these as he had first descended. Wisdom is righteous and clean, but Love is unclean and holy. I sing of the beast and the descent: the great unclean purging itself in fire: the thought that is not born in the measure or the ice or the head, but in the feet and the hot blood and the pulse of fury. The Crown of Life is not lodged in the sun: the wise gods have buried it deeply where the thoughtful will not find it, nor the good: but the Gay Ones, the Adventurous Ones, the Careless Plungers, they will bring it to the wise and astonish them. All things are seen in the light—How shall we value that which is easy to see? But the precious things which are hidden, they will be more precious for our search: they will be beautiful with our sorrow: they will be noble because of our desire for them. Come away with me, Shepherd Girl, through the fields, and we will be careless and happy, and we will leave thought to find us when it can, for that is the duty of thought, and it is more anxious to discover us than we are to be found."

So Caitilin Ni Murrachu arose and went with him through the fields, and she did not go with him because of love, nor because his words had been understood by her, but only because he was naked and unashamed.

Chapter 7

It was on account of his daughter that Meehawl MacMurrachu had come to visit the Philosopher. He did not know what had become of her, and the facts he had to lay before his adviser were very few.

He left the Thin Woman of Inis Magrath taking snuff under a pine tree and went into the house.

"God be with all here," said he as he entered.

"God be with yourself, Meehawl MacMurrachu," said the Philosopher.

"I am in great trouble this day, sir," said Meehawl, "and if you would give me an advice I'd be greatly beholden to you."

"I can give you that," replied the Philosopher.

"None better than your honour and no trouble to you either. It was a powerful advice you gave me about the washboard, and if I didn't come here to thank you before this it was not because I didn't want to come, but that I couldn't move hand or foot by dint of the cruel rheumatism put upon me by the Leprecauns of Gort na Cloca Mora, bad cess to them for ever: twisted I was the way you'd get a squint in your eye if you only looked at me, and the pain I suffered would astonish you."

"It would not," said the Philosopher.

"No matter," said Meehawl. "What I came about was my young daughter Caitilin. Sight or light of her I haven't had for three days. My wife said first, that it was the fairies had taken her, and then she said it was a travelling man that had a musical instrument she went away with, and after that she said, that maybe the girl was lying dead in the butt of a ditch with her eyes wide open, and she staring broadly at the moon in the night time and the sun in the day until the crows would be finding her out."

The Philosopher drew his chair closer to Meehawl.

"Daughters," said he, "have been a cause of anxiety to their parents ever since they were instituted. The flightiness of the female temperament is very evident in those who have not arrived at the years which teach how to hide faults and frailties, and, therefore, indiscretions bristle from a young girl the way branches do from a bush."

"The person who would deny that—" said Meehawl.

"Female children, however, have the particular sanction of nature. They are produced in astonishing excess over males, and may, accordingly, be admitted as dominant to the male; but the well-proven law that the minority shall always control the majority will relieve our minds from a fear which might otherwise become intolerable."

"It's true enough," said Meehawl. "Have you noticed, sir, that in a litter of pups—"

"I have not," said the Philosopher. "Certain trades and professions, it is curious to note, tend to be perpetuated in the female line. The sovereign profession among bees and ants is always female, and publicans also descend on the distaff side. You will have noticed that every publican has three daughters of extraordinary charms. Lacking these signs we would do well to look askance at such a man's liquor, divining that in his brew there will be an undue percentage of water, for if his primogeniture is infected how shall his honesty escape?"

"It would take a wise head to answer that," said Meehawl.

"It would not," said the Philosopher. "Throughout nature the female tends to polygamy."

"If," said Meehawl, "that unfortunate daughter of mine is lying dead in a ditch—"

"It doesn't matter," said the Philosopher. "Many races have endeavoured to place some limits to this increase in females. Certain Oriental peoples have conferred the titles of divinity on crocodiles, serpents, and tigers of the jungle, and have fed these with their surplusage of daughters. In China, likewise, such sacrifices are defended as honourable and economic practices. But, broadly speaking, if daughters have to be curtailed I prefer your method of losing them rather than the religio-hysterical compromises of the Orient."

"I give you my word, sir," said Meehawl, "that I don't know what you are talking about at all."

"That," said the Philosopher, "may be accounted for in three ways—firstly, there is a lack of cerebral continuity: that is, faulty attention; secondly, it might be due to a local peculiarity in the conformation of the skull, or, perhaps, a superficial instead of a deep indenting of the cerebral coil; and thirdly—"

"Did you ever hear," said Meehawl, "of the man that had the scalp of his head blown off by a gun, and they soldered the bottom of a tin dish to the top of his skull the way you could hear his brains ticking inside of it for all the world like a Waterbury watch?"

"I did not," said the Philosopher. "Thirdly, it may—"

"It's my daughter, Caitilin, sir," said Meehawl humbly. "Maybe she is lying in the butt of a ditch and the crows picking her eyes out."

"What did she die of?" said the Philosopher.

"My wife only put it that maybe she was dead, and that maybe she was taken by the fairies, and that maybe she went away with the travelling man that had the musical instrument. She said it was a concertina, but I think myself it was a flute he had."

"Who was this traveller?"

"I never saw him," said Meehawl, "but one day I went a few perches up the hill and I heard him playing—thin, squeaky music it was like you'd be blowing out of a tin whistle. I looked about for him everywhere, but not a bit of him could I see."

"Eh?" said the Philosopher.

"I looked about—" said Meehawl.

"I know," said the Philosopher. "Did you happen to look at your goats?"

"I couldn't well help doing that," said Meehawl.

"What were they doing?" said the Philosopher eagerly.

"They were bucking each other across the field, and standing on their hind legs and cutting such capers that I laughed till I had a pain in my stomach at the gait of them."

"This is very interesting," said the Philosopher.

"Do you tell me so?" said Meehawl.

"I do," said the Philosopher, "and for this reason-most of the races of the world have at one time or another—"

"It's my little daughter, Caitilin, sir," said Meehawl.

"I'm attending to her," the Philosopher replied.

"I thank you kindly," returned Meehawl.

The Philosopher continued "Most of the races of the world have at one time or another been visited by this deity, whose title is the 'Great God Pan,' but there is no record of his ever having journeyed to Ireland, and, certainly within historic times, he has not set foot on these shores. He lived for a great number of years in Egypt, Persia, and Greece, and although his empire is supposed to be world-wide, this universal sway has always been, and always will be, contested; but nevertheless, however sharply his empire may be curtailed, he will never be without a kingdom wherein his exercise of sovereign rights will be gladly and passionately acclaimed."

"Is he one of the old gods, sir?" said Meehawl.

"He is," replied the Philosopher, "and his coming intends no good to this country. Have you any idea why he should have captured your daughter?"

"Not an idea in the world."

"Is your daughter beautiful?"

"I couldn't tell you, because I never thought of looking at her that way. But she is a good milker, and as strong as a man. She can lift a bag of meal under her arm easier than I can; but she's a timid creature for all that."

"Whatever the reason is I am certain that he has the girl, and I am inclined to think that he was directed to her by the Leprecauns of the Gort. You know they are at feud with you ever since their bird was killed?"

"I am not likely to forget it, and they racking me day and night with torments."

"You may be sure," said the Philosopher, "that if he's anywhere at all it's at Gort na Cloca Mora he is, for, being a stranger, he wouldn't know where to go unless he was directed, and they know every hole and corner of this countryside since ancient times. I'd go up myself and have a talk with him, but it wouldn't be a bit of good, and it wouldn't be any use your going either. He has power over all grown people so that they either go and get drunk or else they fall in love with every person they meet, and commit assaults and things I wouldn't like to be telling you about. The only folk who can go near him at all are little children, because he has no power over them until they grow to the sensual age, and then he exercises lordship over them as over every one else. I'll send my two children with a message to him to say that he isn't doing the decent thing, and that if he doesn't let the girl alone and go back to his own country we'll send for Angus Og."

"He'd make short work of him, I'm thinking."

"He might surely; but he may take the girl for himself all the same."

"Well, I'd sooner he had her than the other one, for he's one of ourselves anyhow, and the devil you know is better than the devil you don't know."

"Angus Og is a god," said the Philosopher severely.

"I know that, sir," replied Meehawl; "it's only a way of talking I have. But how will your honour get at Angus? for I heard say that he hadn't been seen for a hundred years, except one night only when he talked to a man for half an hour on Kilmasheogue."

"I'll find him, sure enough," replied the Philosopher.

"I'll warrant you will," replied Meehawl heartily as he stood up. "Long life and good health to your honour," said he as he turned away.

The Philosopher lit his pipe.

"We live as long as we are let," said he, "and we get the health we deserve. Your salutation embodies a reflection on death which is not philosophic. We must acquiesce in all logical progressions. The merging of opposites is completion. Life runs to death as to its goal, and we should go towards that next stage of experience either carelessly as to what must be, or with a good, honest curiosity as to what may be."

"There's not much fun in being dead, sir," said Meehawl.

"How do you know?" said the Philosopher.

"I know well enough," replied Meehawl.

Chapter 8

When the children leaped into the hole at the foot of the tree they found themselves sliding down a dark, narrow slant which dropped them softly enough into a little room. This room was hollowed out immediately under the tree, and great care had been taken not to disturb any of the roots which ran here and there through the chamber in the strangest criss-cross, twisted fashion. To get across such a place one had to walk round, and jump over, and duck under perpetually. Some of the roots had formed themselves very conveniently into low seats and narrow, uneven tables, and at the bottom all the roots ran into the floor and away again in the direction required by their business. After the clear air outside this place was very dark to the children's eyes, so that they could not see anything for a few minutes, but after a little time their eyes became accustomed to the semiobscurity and they were able to see quite well. The first things they became aware of were six small men who were seated on low roots. They were all dressed in tight green clothes and little leathern aprons, and they wore tall green hats which wobbled when they moved. They were all busily engaged making shoes. One was drawing out wax ends on his knee, another was softening pieces of leather in a bucket of water, another was polishing the instep of a shoe with a piece of curved bone, another was paring down a heel with a short broad-bladed knife, and another was hammering wooden pegs into a sole. He had all the pegs in his mouth, which gave him a widefaced, jolly expression, and according as a peg was wanted he blew it into his hand and hit it twice with his hammer, and then he blew another peg, and he always blew the peg with the right end uppermost, and never had to hit it more than twice. He was a person well worth watching.

The children had slid down so unexpectedly that they almost forgot their good manners, but as soon as Seumas Beg discovered that he was really in a room he removed his cap and stood up.

"God be with all here," said he.

The Leprecaun who had brought them lifted Brigid from the floor to which amazement still constrained her.

"Sit down on that little root, child of my heart," said he, "and you can knit stockings for us."

"Yes, sir," said Brigid meekly.

The Leprecaun took four knitting needles and a ball of green wool from the top of a high, horizontal root. He had to climb over one, go round three and climb up two roots to get at it, and he did this so easily that it did not seem a bit of trouble. He gave the needles and wool to Brigid Beg.

"Do you know how to turn the heel, Brigid Beg?" said he.

"No, sir," said Brigid.

"Well, I'll show you how when you come to it."

The other six Leprecauns had ceased work and were looking at the children. Seumas turned to them.

"God bless the work," said he politely.

One of the Leprecauns, who had a grey, puckered face and a thin fringe of grey whisker very far under his chin, then spoke.

"Come over here, Seumas Beg," said he, "and I'll measure you for a pair of shoes. Put your foot up on that root."

The boy did so, and the Leprecaun took the measure of his foot with a wooden rule.

"Now, Brigid Beg, show me your foot," and he measured her also. "They'll be ready for you in the morning."

"Do you never do anything else but make shoes, sir?" said Seumas.

"We do not," replied the Leprecaun, "except when we want new clothes, and then we have to make them, but we grudge every minute spent making anything else except shoes, because that is the proper work for a Leprecaun. In the night time we go about the country into people's houses and we clip little pieces off their money, and so, bit by bit, we get a crock of gold together, because, do you see, a Leprecaun has to have a crock of gold so that if he's captured by men folk he may be able to ransom himself. But that seldom happens, because it's a great disgrace altogether to be captured by a man, and we've practiced so long dodging among the roots here that we can easily get away from them. Of course, now and again we are caught; but men are fools, and we always escape without having to pay the ransom at all. We wear green clothes because it's the colour of the grass and the leaves, and when we sit down under a bush or lie in the grass they just walk by without noticing us."

"Will you let me see your crock of gold?" said Seumas.

The Leprecaun looked at him fixedly for a moment.

"Do you like griddle bread and milk?" said he.

"I like it well," Seumas answered.

"Then you had better have some," and the Leprecaun took a piece of griddle bread from the shelf and filled two saucers with milk.

While the children were eating the Leprecauns asked them many questions "What time do you get up in the morning?"

"Seven o'clock," replied Seumas.

"And what do you have for breakfast?"

"Stirabout and milk," he replied.

"It's good food," said the Leprecaun. "What do you have for dinner?"

"Potatoes and milk," said Seumas.

"It's not bad at all," said the Leprecaun. "And what do you have for supper?"

Brigid answered this time because her brother's mouth was full.

"Bread and milk, sir," said she.

"There's nothing better," said the Leprecaun.

"And then we go to bed," continued Brigid.

"Why wouldn't you?" said the Leprecaun.

It was at this point the Thin Woman of Inis Magrath knocked on the tree trunk and demanded that the children should be returned to her.

When she had gone away the Leprecauns held a consultation, whereat it was decided that they could not afford to anger the Thin Woman and the Shee of Croghan Conghaile, so they shook hands with the children and bade them good-bye. The Leprecaun who had enticed them away from home brought them back again, and on parting he begged the children to visit Gort na Cloca Mora whenever they felt inclined.

"There's always a bit of griddle bread or potato cake, and a noggin of milk for a friend," said he.

"You are very kind, sir," replied Seumas, and his sister said the same words.

As the Leprecaun walked away they stood watching him.

"Do you remember," said Seumas, "the way he hopped and waggled his leg the last time he was here?"

"I do so," replied Brigid.

"Well, he isn't hopping or doing anything at all this time," said Seumas.

"He's not in good humour to-night," said Brigid, "but I like him."

"So do I," said Seumas.

When they went into the house the Thin Woman of Inis Magrath was very glad to see them, and she baked a cake with currants in it, and also gave them both stir-about and potatoes; but the Philosopher did not notice that they had been away at all. He said at last that "talking was bad wit, that women were always making a fuss, that children should be fed, but not fattened, and that beds were meant to be slept in." The Thin Woman replied "that he was a grisly old man without bowels, that she did not know what she had married him for, that he was three times her age, and that no one would believe what she had to put up with."

Chapter 9

Pursuant to his arrangement with Meehawl MacMurrachu, the Philosopher sent the children in search of Pan. He gave them the fullest instructions as to how they should address the Sylvan Deity, and then, having received the admonishments of the Thin Woman of Inis Magrath, the children departed in the early morning.

When they reached the clearing in the pine wood, through which the sun was blazing, they sat down for a little while to rest in the heat. Birds were continually darting down this leafy shaft, and diving away into the dark wood. These birds always had something in their beaks. One would have a worm, or a snail, or a grasshopper, or a little piece of wool torn off a sheep, or a scrap of cloth, or a piece of hay; and when they had put these things in a certain place they flew up the sun-shaft again and looked for something else to bring home. On seeing the children each of the birds waggled his wings, and made a particular sound. They said "caw" and "chip" and "twit" and "tut" and "what" and "pit"; and one, whom the youngsters liked very much, always said "tit-tittit-tit-tit." The children were fond of him because he was so all-of-asudden. They never knew where he was going to fly next, and they did not believe he knew himself. He would fly backwards and forwards, and up and down, and sideways and bawways—all, so to speak, in the one breath. He did this because he was curious to see what was happening everywhere, and, as something is always happening everywhere, he was never able to fly in a straight line for more than the littlest distance. He was a cowardly bird too, and continually fancied that some person was going to throw a stone at him from behind a bush, or a wall, or a tree, and these imaginary dangers tended to make his journeyings still more wayward and erratic. He never flew where he wanted to go himself, but only where God directed him, and so he did not fare at all badly.

The children knew each of the birds by their sounds, and always said these words to them when they came near. For a little time they had difficulty in saying the right word to the right bird, and sometimes said "chip" when the salutation should have been "tut." The birds always resented this, and would scold them angrily, but after a little practice they never made any mistakes at all. There was one bird, a big, black fellow, who loved to be talked to. He used to sit on the ground beside the children, and say "caw" as long as they would repeat it after him.

He often wasted a whole morning in talk, but none of the other birds remained for more than a few minutes at a time. They were always busy in the morning, but in the evening they had more leisure, and would stay and chat as long as the children wanted them. The awkward thing was that in the evening all the birds wanted to talk at the same moment, so that the youngsters never knew which of them to answer. Seumas Beg got out of that difficulty for a while by learning to whistle their notes, but, even so, they spoke with such rapidity that he could not by any means keep pace with them. Brigid could only whistle one note; it was a little flat "whoo" sound, which the birds all laughed at, and after a few trials she refused to whistle any more.

While they were sitting two rabbits came to play about in the brush. They ran round and round in a circle, and all their movements were very quick and twisty. Sometimes they jumped over each other six or seven times in succession, and every now and then they sat upright on their hind legs, and washed their faces with their paws. At other times they picked up a blade of grass, which they ate with great deliberation, pretending all the time that it was a complicated banquet of cabbage leaves and lettuce.

While the children were playing with the rabbits an ancient, stalwart he-goat came prancing through the bracken. He was an old acquaintance of theirs, and he enjoyed lying beside them to have his forehead scratched with a piece of sharp stick. His forehead was hard as rock, and the hair grew there as sparse as grass does on a wall, or rather the way moss grows on a wall—it was a mat instead of a crop. His horns were long and very sharp, and brilliantly polished. On this day the he-goat had two chains around his neck—one was made of buttercups and the other was made of daisies, and the children wondered to each other who it was could have woven these so carefully. They asked the he-goat this question, but he only looked at them and did not say a word. The children liked examining this goat's eyes; they were very big, and of the queerest light-gray colour. They had a strange steadfast look, and had also at times a look of queer, deep intelligence, and at other times they had a fatherly and benevolent expression, and at other times again, especially when he looked sidewards, they had a mischievous, light-and-airy, daring, mocking, inviting and terrifying look; but he always looked brave and unconcerned. When the he-goat's forehead had been scratched as much as he desired he arose from between the children and went pacing away lightly through the wood. The children ran after him and each caught hold of one of his horns, and he ambled and reared between them while they danced along on his either side singing snatches of bird songs, and scraps of old tunes which the Thin Woman of Inis Magrath had learned among the people of the Shee.

In a little time they came to Gort na Cloca Mora, but here the he-goat did not stop. They went past the big tree of the Leprecauns, through a broken part of the hedge and into another rough field. The sun was shining gloriously. There was scarcely a wind at all to stir the harsh grasses. Far and near was silence and warmth, an immense, cheerful peace. Across the sky a few light clouds sailed gently on a blue so vast that the eye failed before that horizon. A few bees sounded their deep chant, and now and again a wasp rasped hastily on his journey. Than these there was no sound of any kind. So peaceful, innocent and safe did everything appear that it might have been the childhood of the world as it was of the morning.

The children, still clinging to the friendly goat, came near the edge of the field, which here sloped more steeply to the mountain top. Great boulders, slightly covered with lichen and moss, were strewn about, and around them the bracken and gorse were growing, and in every crevice of these rocks there were plants whose little, tight-fisted roots gripped a desperate, adventurous habitation in a soil scarcely more than half an inch deep. At some time these rocks had been smitten so fiercely that the solid granite surfaces had shattered into fragments. At one place a sheer wall of stone, ragged and battered, looked harshly out from the thin vegetation. To this rocky wall the he-goat danced. At one place there was a hole in the wall covered by a thick brush. The goat pushed his way behind this growth and disappeared. Then the children, curious to see where he had gone, pushed through also. Behind the bush they found a high, narrow opening, and when they had rubbed their legs, which smarted from the stings of nettles, thistles and gorse prickles, they went into the hole which they thought was a place the goat had for sleeping in on cold, wet nights. After a few paces they found the passage was quite comfortably big, and then they saw a light, and in another moment they were blinking at the god Pan and Caitilin Ni Murrachu.

Caitilin knew them at once and came forward with welcome.

"O, Seumas Beg," she cried reproachfully, "how dirty you have let your feet get. Why don't you walk in the grassy places? And you, Brigid, have a right to be ashamed of yourself to have your hands the way they are. Come over here at once."

Every child knows that every grown female person in the world has authority to wash children and to give them food; that is what grown people were made for, consequently Seumas and Brigid Beg submitted to the scouring for which Caitilin made instant preparation. When they were cleaned she pointed to a couple of flat stones against the wall of the cave and bade them sit down and be good, and this the children did, fixing their eyes on Pan with the cheerful gravity and curiosity which good-natured youngsters always give to a stranger.

Pan, who had been lying on a couch of dried grass, sat up and bent an equally cheerful regard on the children.

"Shepherd Girl," said he, "who are those children?"

"They are the children of the Philosophers of Coilla Doraca; the Grey Woman of Dun Gortin and the Thin Woman of Inis Magrath are their mothers, and they are decent, poor children, God bless them."

"What have they come here for?"

"You will have to ask themselves that."

Pan looked at them smilingly.

"What have you come here for, little children?" said he.

The children questioned one another with their eyes to see which of them would reply, and then Seumas Beg answered:

"My father sent me to see you, sir, and to say that you were not doing a good thing in keeping Caitilin Ni Murrachu away from her own place."

Brigid Beg turned to Caitilin—

"Your father came to see our father, and he said that he didn't know what had become of you at all, and that maybe you were lying flat in a ditch with the black crows picking at your flesh."

"And what," said Pan, "did your father say to that?"

"He told us to come and ask her to go home."

"Do you love your father, little child?" said Pan.

Brigid Beg thought for a moment. "I don't know, sir," she replied.

"He doesn't mind us at all," broke in Seumas Beg, "and so we don't know whether we love him or not."

"I like Caitilin," said Brigid, "and I like you."

"So do I," said Seumas.

"I like you also, little children," said Pan. "Come over here and sit beside me, and we will talk."

So the two children went over to Pan and sat down one each side of him, and he put his arms about them. "Daughter of Murrachu," said he, "is there no food in the house for guests?"

"There is a cake of bread, a little goat's milk and some cheese," she replied, and she set about getting these things.

"I never ate cheese," said Seumas. "Is it good?"

"Surely it is," replied Pan. "The cheese that is made from goat's milk is rather strong, and it is good to be eaten by people who live in the open air, but not by those who live in houses, for such people do not have any appetite. They are poor creatures whom I do not like."

"I like eating," said Seumas.

"So do I," said Pan. "All good people like eating. Every person who is hungry is a good person, and every person who is not hungry is a bad person. It is better to be hungry than rich."

Caitilin having supplied the children with food, seated herself in front of them. "I don't think that is right," said she. "I have always been hungry, and it was never good."

"If you had always been full you would like it even less," he replied, "because when you are hungry you are alive, and when you are not hungry you are only half alive."

"One has to be poor to be hungry," replied Caitilin. "My father is poor and gets no good of it but to work from morning to night and never to stop doing that."

"It is bad for a wise person to be poor," said Pan, "and it is bad for a fool to be rich. A rich fool will think of nothing else at first but to find a dark house wherein to hide away, and there he will satisfy his hunger, and he will continue to do that until his hunger is dead and he is no better than dead but a wise person who is rich will carefully preserve his appetite. All people who have been rich for a long time, or who are rich from birth, live a great deal outside of their houses, and so they are always hungry and healthy."

"Poor people have no time to be wise," said Caitilin.

"They have time to be hungry," said Pan. "I ask no more of them."

"My father is very wise," said Seumas Beg.

"How do you know that, little boy?" said Pan.

"Because he is always talking," replied Seumas. "Do you always listen, my dear?"

"No, sir," said Seumas; "I go to sleep when he talks."

"That is very clever of you," said Pan.

"I go to sleep too," said Brigid.

"It is clever of you also, my darling. Do you go to sleep when your mother talks?"

"Oh, no," she answered. "If we went to sleep then our mother would pinch us and say that we were a bad breed."

"I think your mother is wise," said Pan. "What do you like best in the world, Seumas Beg?"

The boy thought for a moment and replied: "I don't know, sir."

Pan also thought for a little time.

"I don't know what I like best either," said he. "What do you like best in the world, Shepherd Girl?"

Caitilin's eyes were fixed on his.

"I don't know yet," she answered slowly.

"May the gods keep you safe from that knowledge," said Pan gravely.

"Why would you say that?" she replied. "One must find out all things, and when we find out a thing we know if it is good or bad."

"That is the beginning of knowledge," said Pan, "but it is not the beginning of wisdom."

"What is the beginning of wisdom?"

"It is carelessness," replied Pan.

"And what is the end of wisdom?" said she.

"I do not know," he answered, after a little pause.

"Is it greater carelessness?" she enquired.

"I do not know, I do not know," said he sharply. "I am tired of talking," and, so saying, he turned his face away from them and lay down on the couch.

Caitilin in great concern hurried the children to the door of the cave and kissed them good-bye.

"Pan is sick," said the boy gravely.

"I hope he will be well soon again," the girl murmured.

"Yes, yes," said Caitilin, and she ran back quickly to her lord.

BOOK 2
THE PHILOSOPHER'S JOURNEY

Chapter 10

When the children reached home they told the Philosopher—the result of their visit. He questioned them minutely as to the appearance of Pan, how he had received them, and what he had said in defence of his iniquities; but when he found that Pan had not returned any answer to his message he became very angry. He tried to persuade his wife to undertake another embassy setting forth his abhorrence and defiance of the god, but the Thin Woman replied sourly that she was a respectable married woman, that having been already bereaved of her wisdom she had no desire to be further curtailed of her virtue, that a husband would go any length to asperse his wife's reputation, and that although she was married to a fool her self-respect had survived even that calamity. The Philosopher pointed out that her age, her appearance, and her tongue were sufficient guarantees of immunity against the machinations of either Pan or slander, and that he had no personal feelings in the matter beyond a scientific and benevolent interest in the troubles of Meehawl MacMurrachu; but this was discounted by his wife as the malignant and subtle tactics customary to all husbands.

Matters appeared to be thus at a deadlock so far as they were immediately concerned, and the Philosopher decided that he would lay the case before Angus Og and implore his protection and assistance on behalf of the Clann MacMurrachu. He therefore directed the Thin Woman to bake him two cakes of bread, and set about preparations for a journey.

The Thin Woman baked the cakes, and put them in a bag, and early on the following morning the Philosopher swung this bag over his shoulder, and went forth on his quest.

When he came to the edge of the pine wood he halted for a few moments, not being quite certain of his bearings, and then went forward again in the direction of Gort na Cloca Mora. It came into his mind as he crossed the Gort that he ought to call on the Leprecauns and have a talk with them, but a remembrance of Meehawl MacMurrachu and the troubles under which he laboured (all directly to be traced to the Leprecauns) hardened his heart against his neighbours, so that he passed by the yew tree without any stay. In a short time he came to the rough, heather-clumped field wherein the children had found Pan, and as he was proceeding up the hill, he saw Caitilin Ni Murrachu walking a little way in front with a small vessel in her hand. The she-goat which she had just milked was bending again to the herbage, and as Caitilin trod lightly in front of him the Philosopher closed his eyes in virtuous anger and opened them again in a not unnatural curiosity, for the girl had no clothes on. He watched her going behind the brush and disappearing in the cleft of the rock, and his anger, both with her and Pan, mastering him he forsook the path of prudence which soared to the mountain top, and followed that leading to the cave. The sound of his feet brought Caitilin out hastily, but he pushed her by with a harsh word. "Hussy," said he, and he went into the cave where Pan was.

As he went in he already repented of his harshness and said "The human body is an aggregation of flesh and sinew, around a central bony structure. The use of clothing is primarily to protect this organism from rain and cold, and it may not be regarded as the banner of morality without danger to this fundamental premise. If a person does not desire to be so protected who will quarrel with an honourable liberty? Decency is not clothing but Mind. Morality is behaviour. Virtue is thought; I have often fancied," he continued to Pan, whom he was now confronting, "that the effect of clothing on mind must be very considerable, and that it must have a modifying rather than an expanding effect, or, even, an intensifying as against an exuberant effect. With clothing the whole environment is immediately affected. The air, which is our proper medium, is only filtered to our bodies in an abated and niggardly fashion which can scarcely be as beneficial as the generous and unintermitted elemental play. The question naturally arises whether clothing is as unknown to nature as we have fancied? Viewed as a protective measure against atmospheric rigour we find that many creatures grow, by their own central impulse, some kind of exterior panoply which may be regarded as their proper clothing. Bears, cats, dogs, mice, sheep and beavers are wrapped in fur, hair, fell, fleece or pelt, so these creatures cannot by any means be regarded as being naked. Crabs, cockroaches, snails and cockles have ordered around them a crusty habiliment, wherein their original nakedness is only to be discovered by force, and other creatures have similarly provided themselves with some species of covering. Clothing, therefore, is not an art, but an instinct, and the fact that man is born naked and does not grow his clothing upon himself from within but collects it from various distant and haphazard sources is not any reason to call this necessity an instinct for decency. These, you will admit, are weighty reflections and worthy of consideration before we proceed to the wide and thorny subject of moral and immoral action. Now, what is virtue?" Pan, who had listened with great courtesy to these remarks, here broke in on the Philosopher.

"Virtue," said he, "is the performance of pleasant actions."

The Philosopher held the statement for a moment on his forefinger.

"And what, then, is vice?" said he.

"It is vicious," said Pan, "to neglect the performance of pleasant actions."

"If this be so," the other commented, "philosophy has up to the present been on the wrong track."

"That is so," said Pan. "Philosophy is an immoral practice because it suggests a standard of practice impossible of being followed, and which, if it could be followed, would lead to the great sin of sterility."

"The idea of virtue," said the Philosopher, with some indignation, "has animated the noblest intellects of the world."

"It has not animated them," replied Pan; "it has hypnotised them so that they have conceived virtue as repression and self-sacrifice as an honourable thing instead of the suicide which it is."

"Indeed," said the Philosopher; "this is very interesting, and if it is true the whole conduct of life will have to be very much simplified."

"Life is already very simple," said Pan; "it is to be born and to die, and in the interval to eat and drink, to dance and sing, to marry and beget children."

"But it is simply materialism," cried the Philosopher.

"Why do you say 'but'?" replied Pan.

"It is sheer, unredeemed animalism," continued his visitor.

"It is any name you please to call it," replied Pan.

"You have proved nothing," the Philosopher shouted.

"What can be sensed requires no proof."

"You leave out the new thing," said the Philosopher. "You leave out brains. I believe in mind above matter. Thought above emotion. Spirit above flesh."

"Of course you do," said Pan, and he reached for his oaten pipe.

The Philosopher ran to the opening of the passage and thrust Caitilin aside. "Hussy," said he fiercely to her, and he darted out.

As he went up the rugged path he could hear the pipes of Pan, calling and sobbing and making high merriment on the air.

Chapter 11

S he does not deserve to be rescued," said the Philosopher, "but I will rescue her. Indeed," he thought a moment later, "she does not want to be rescued, and, therefore, I will rescue her."

As he went down the road her shapely figure floated before his eyes as beautiful and simple as an old statue. He wagged his head angrily at the apparition, but it would not go away. He tried to concentrate his mind on a deep, philosophical maxim, but her disturbing image came between him and his thought, blotting out the latter so completely that a moment after he had stated his aphorism he could not remember what it had been. Such a condition of mind was so unusual that it bewildered him.

"Is a mind, then, so unstable," said he, "that a mere figure, an animated geometrical arrangement can shake it from its foundations?"

The idea horrified him: he saw civilisation building its temples over a volcano. . .

"A puff," said he, "and it is gone. Beneath all is chaos and red anarchy, over all a devouring and insistent appetite. Our eyes tell us what to think about, and our wisdom is no more than a catalogue of sensual stimuli."

He would have been in a state of deep dejection were it not that through his perturbation there bubbled a stream of such amazing well-being as he had not felt since childhood. Years had toppled from his shoulders. He left one pound of solid matter behind at every stride. His very skin grew flexuous, and he found a pleasure in taking long steps such as he could not have accounted for by thought. Indeed, thought was the one thing he felt unequal to, and it was not precisely that he could not think but that he did not want to. All the importance and authority of his mind seemed to have faded away, and the activity which had once belonged to that organ was now transferred to his eyes. He saw, amazedly, the sunshine bathing the hills and the valleys. A bird in the hedge held him—beak, head, eyes, legs, and the wings that tapered widely at angles to the wind. For the first time in his life he really saw a bird, and one minute after it had flown away he could have reproduced its strident note. With every step along the curving road the landscape was changing. He saw and noted it almost in an ecstasy. A sharp hill jutted out into the road, it dissolved into a sloping meadow, rolled down into a valley and then climbed easily and peacefully into a hill again. On this side a clump of trees nodded together in the friendliest fashion. Yonder a solitary tree, well-grown and clean, was contented with its own bright company. A bush crouched tightly on the ground as though, at a word, it would scamper from its place and chase rabbits across the sward with shouts and laughter. Great spaces of sunshine were everywhere, and everywhere there were deep wells of shadow; and the one did not seem more beautiful than the other. That sunshine! Oh, the glory of it, the goodness and bravery of it, how broadly and grandly it shone, without stint, without care; he saw its measureless generosity and gloried in it as though himself had been the flinger of that largesse. And was he not? Did the sunlight not stream from his head and life from his finger-tips? Surely the well-being that was in him did bubble out to an activity beyond the universe. Thought! Oh! the petty thing! but motion! emotion! these were the realities. To feel, to do, to stride forward in elation chanting a paean of triumphant life!

After a time he felt hungry, and thrusting his hand into his wallet he broke off a piece of one of his cakes and looked about for a place where he might happily eat it. By the side of the road there was a well; just a little corner filled with water. Over it was a rough stone coping, and around, hugging it on three sides almost from sight, were thick, quiet bushes. He would not have noticed the well at all but for a thin stream, the breadth of two hands, which tiptoed away from it through a field. By this well he sat down and scooped the water in his hand and it tasted good.

He was eating his cake when a sound touched his ear from some distance, and shortly a woman came down the path carrying a vessel in her hand to draw water.

She was a big, comely woman, and she walked as one who had no misfortunes and no misgivings. When she saw the Philosopher sitting by the well she halted a moment in surprise and then came forward with a good-humoured smile.

"Good morrow to you, sir," said she.

"Good morrow to you too, ma'am," replied the Philosopher. "Sit down beside me here and eat some of my cake."

"Why wouldn't I, indeed," said the woman, and she did sit beside him.

The Philosopher cracked a large piece off his cake and gave it to her and she ate some.

"There's a taste on that cake," said she. "Who made it?"

"My wife did," he replied.

"Well, now!" said she, looking at him. "Do you know, you don't look a bit like a married man."

"No?" said the Philosopher.

"Not a bit. A married man looks comfortable and settled: he looks finished, if you understand me, and a bachelor looks unsettled and funny, and he always wants to be running round seeing things. I'd know a married man from a bachelor any day."

"How would you know that?" said the Philosopher.

"Easily," said she, with a nod. "It's the way they look at a woman. A married man looks at you quietly as if he knew all about you. There isn't any strangeness about him with a woman at all; but a bachelor man looks at you very sharp and looks away and then looks back again, the way you'd know he was thinking about you and didn't know what you were thinking about him; and so they are always strange, and that's why women like them."

"Why!" said the Philosopher, astonished, "do women like bachelors better than married men?"

"Of course they do," she replied heartily. "They wouldn't look at the side of the road a married man was on if there was a bachelor man on the other side."

"This," said the Philosopher earnestly, "is very interesting."

"And the queer thing is," she continued, "that when I came up the road and saw you I said to myself 'it's a bachelor man.' How long have you been married, now?"

"I don't know," said the Philosopher. "Maybe it's ten years."

"And how many children would you have, mister?"

"Two," he replied, and then corrected himself, "No, I have only one."

"Is the other one dead?"

"I never had more than one."

"Ten years married and only one child," said she. "Why, man dear, you're not a married man. What were you doing at all, at all! I wouldn't like to be telling you the children I have living and dead. But what I say is that married or not you're a bachelor man. I knew it the minute I looked at you. What sort of a woman is herself?"

"She's a thin sort of woman," cried the Philosopher, biting into his cake.

"Is she now?"

"And," the Philosopher continued, "the reason I talked to you is because you are a fat woman."

"I am not fat," was her angry response.

"You are fat," insisted the Philosopher, "and that's the reason I like you."

"Oh, if you mean it that way. . ." she chuckled.

"I think," he continued, looking at her admiringly, "that women ought to be fat."

"Tell you the truth," said she eagerly, "I think that myself. I never met a thin woman but she was a sour one, and I never met a fat man but he was a fool. Fat women and thin men; it's nature," said she.

"It is," said he, and he leaned forward and kissed her eye.

"Oh, you villain!" said the woman, putting out her hands against him.

The Philosopher drew back abashed. "Forgive me," he began, "if I have alarmed your virtue—"

"It's the married man's word," said she, rising hastily: "now I know you; but there's a lot of the bachelor in you all the same, God help you! I'm going home." And, so saying, she dipped her vessel in the well and turned away.

"Maybe," said the Philosopher, "I ought to wait until your husband comes home and ask his forgiveness for the wrong I've done him."

The woman turned round on him and each of her eyes was as big as a plate.

"What do you say?" said she. "Follow me if you dare and I'll set the dog on you; I will so," and she strode viciously homewards.

After a moment's hesitation the Philosopher took his own path across the hill.

The day was now well advanced, and as he trudged forward the happy quietude of his surroundings stole into his heart again and so toned down his recollection of the fat woman that in a little time she was no more than a pleasant and curious memory. His mind was exercised superficially, not in thinking, but in wondering how it was he had come to kiss a strange woman. He said to himself that such conduct was not right; but this statement was no more than the automatic working of a mind long exercised in the distinctions of right and wrong, for, almost in the same breath, he assured himself that what he had done did not matter in the least. His opinions were undergoing a curious change. Right and wrong were meeting and blending together so closely that it became difficult to dissever them, and the obloquy attaching to the one seemed out of proportion altogether to its importance, while the other by no means justified the eulogy wherewith it was connected. Was there any immediate or even distant, effect on life caused by evil which was not instantly swung into equipoise by goodness? But these slender reflections troubled him only for a little time. He had little desire for any introspective quarryings. To feel so well was sufficient in itself. Why should thought be so apparent to us, so insistent? We do not know we have digestive or circulatory organs until these go out of order, and then the knowledge torments us. Should not the labours of a healthy brain be equally subterranean and equally competent? Why have we to think aloud and travel laboriously from syllogism to ergo, chary of our conclusions and distrustful of our premises? Thought, as we know it, is a disease and no more. The healthy mentality should register its convictions and not its labours. Our ears should not hear the clamour of its doubts nor be forced to listen to the pro and con wherewith we are eternally badgered and perplexed.

The road was winding like a ribbon in and out of the mountains. On either side there were hedges and bushes,—little, stiff trees which held their foliage in their hands and dared the winds snatch a leaf from that grip. The hills were swelling and sinking, folding and soaring on every view. Now the silence was startled by the falling tinkle of a stream. Far away a cow lowed, a long, deep monotone, or a goat's call trembled from nowhere to nowhere. But mostly there was a silence which buzzed with a multitude of small winged life. Going up the hills the Philosopher bent forward to the gradient, stamping vigorously as he trod, almost snorting like a bull in the pride of successful energy. Coming down the slope he braced back and let his legs loose to do as they pleased. Didn't they know their business—Good luck to them, and away!

As he walked along he saw an old woman hobbling in front of him. She was leaning on a stick and her hand was red and swollen with rheumatism. She hobbled by reason of the fact that there were stones in her shapeless boots. She was draped in the sorriest miscellaneous rags that could be imagined, and these were knotted together so intricately that her clothing, having once been attached to her body, could never again be detached from it. As she walked she was mumbling and grumbling to herself, so that her mouth moved round and round in an india-rubber fashion.

The Philosopher soon caught up on her.

"Good morrow, ma'am," said he.

But she did not hear him: she seemed to be listening to the pain which the stones in her boots gave her.

"Good morrow, ma'am," said the Philosopher again.

This time she heard him and replied, turning her old, bleared eyes slowly in his direction—

"Good morrow to yourself, sir," said she, and the Philosopher thought her old face was a very kindly one.

"What is it that is wrong with you, ma'am?" said he.

"It's my boots, sir," she replied. "Full of stones they are, the way I can hardly walk at all, God help me!"

"Why don't you shake them out?"

"Ah, sure, I couldn't be bothered, sir, for there are so many holes in the boots that more would get in before I could take two steps, and an old woman can't be always fidgeting, God help her!"

There was a little house on one side of the road, and when the old woman saw this place she brightened up a little.

"Do you know who lives in that house?" said the Philosopher.

"I do not," she replied, "but it's a real nice house with clean windows and a shiny knocker on the door, and smoke in the chimney—I wonder would herself give me a cup of tea now if I asked her—A poor old woman walking the roads on a stick! and maybe a bit of meat, or an egg perhaps. . ."

"You could ask," suggested the Philosopher gently.

"Maybe I will, too," said she, and she sat down by the road just outside the house and the Philosopher also sat down.

A little puppy dog came from behind the house and approached them cautiously. Its intentions were friendly but it had already found that amicable advances are sometimes indifferently received, for, as it drew near, it wagged its dubious tail and rolled humbly on the ground. But very soon the dog discovered that here there was no evil, for it trotted over to the old woman, and without any more preparation jumped into her lap.

The old woman grinned at the dog "Ah, you thing you!" said she, and she gave it her finger to bite. The delighted puppy chewed her bony finger, and then instituted a mimic warfare against a piece of rag that fluttered from her breast, barking and growling in joyous excitement, while the old woman fondled and hugged it.

The door of the house opposite opened quickly, and a woman with a frost-bitten face came out.

"Leave that dog down," said she.

The old woman grinned humbly at her.

"Sure, ma'am, I wouldn't hurt the little dog, the thing!"

"Put down that dog," said the woman, "and go about your business—the likes of you ought to be arrested."

A man in shirt sleeves appeared behind her, and at him the old woman grinned even more humbly.

"Let me sit here for a while and play with the little dog, sir," said she; "sure the roads do be lonesome—"

The man stalked close and grabbed the dog by the scruff of the neck. It hung between his finger and thumb with its tail tucked between its legs and its eyes screwed round on one side in amazement.

"Be off with you out of that, you old strap!" said the man in a terrible voice.

So the old woman rose painfully to her feet again, and as she went hobbling along the dusty road she began to cry.

The Philosopher also arose; he was very indignant but did not know what to do. A singular lassitude also prevented him from interfering. As they paced along his companion began mumbling, more to herself than to him "Ah, God be with me," said she, "an old woman on a stick, that hasn't a place in the wide world to go to or a neighbour itself. . . I wish I could get a cup of tea, so I do. I wish to God I could get a cup of tea. . . Me sitting down in my own little house, with the white tablecloth on the table, and the butter in the dish, and the strong, red tea in the tea-cup; and me pouring cream into it, and, maybe, telling the children not to be wasting the sugar, the things! and himself saying he'd got to mow the big field to-day, or that the red cow was going to calve, the poor thing, and that if the boys went to school, who was going to weed the turnips—and me sitting drinking my strong cup of tea, and telling him where that old trapesing hen was laying. . . Ah, God be with me! an old creature hobbling along the roads on a stick. I wish I was a young girl again, so I do, and himself coming courting me, and him saying that I was a real nice little girl surely, and that nothing would make him happy or easy at all but me to be loving him.—Ah, the kind man that he was, to be sure, the kind, decent man. . . And Sorca Reilly to be trying to get him from me, and Kate Finnegan with her bold eyes looking after him in the Chapel; and him to be saying that along with me they were only a pair of old nanny goats. . . And then me to be getting married and going home to my own little house with my man—ah, God be with me! and him kissing me, and laughing, and frightening me with his goings-on. Ah, the kind man, with his soft eyes, and his nice voice, and his jokes and laughing, and him thinking the world and all of me—ay, indeed. . . And the neighbours to be coming in and sitting round the fire in the night time, putting the world through each other, and talking about France and Russia and them other queer places, and him holding up the discourse like a learned man, and them all listening to him and nodding their heads at each other, and wondering at his education and all: or, maybe, the neighbours to be singing, or him making me sing the Coulin, and him to be proud of me. . . and then him to be killed on me with a cold on his chest. . . Ah, then, God be with me, a lone, old creature on a stick, and the sun shining into her eyes and she thirsty—I wish I had a cup of tea, so I do. I wish to God I had a cup of tea and a bit of meat. . . or, maybe, an egg. A nice fresh egg laid by the speckeldy hen that used to be giving me all the trouble, the thing! . . . Sixteen hens I had, and they were the ones for laying, surely. . . It's the queer world, so it is, the queer world—and the things that do happen for no reason at all. . . Ah, God be with me! I wish there weren't stones in my boots, so I do, and I wish to God I had a cup of tea and a fresh egg. Ah, glory be, my old legs are getting tireder every day, so they are. Wisha, one time—when himself was in it—I could go about the house all day long, cleaning the place, and feeding the pigs, and the hens and all, and then dance half the night, so I could: and himself proud of me. . ."

The old woman turned up a little rambling road and went on still talking to herself, and the Philosopher watched her go up that road for a long time. He was very glad she had gone away, and as he tramped forward he banished her sad image so that in a little time he was happy again. The sun was still shining, the birds were flying on every side, and the wide hill-side above him smiled gaily.

A small, narrow road cut at right angles into his path, and as he approached this he heard the bustle and movement of a host, the trample of feet, the rolling and creaking of wheels, and the long unwearied drone of voices. In a few minutes he came abreast of this small road, and saw an ass and cart piled with pots and pans, and walking beside this there were two men and a woman. The men and the woman were talking together loudly, even fiercely, and the ass was drawing his cart along the road without requiring assistance or direction. While there was a road he walked on it: when he might come to a cross road he would turn to the right: when a man said "whoh" he would stop: when he said "hike" he would go backwards, and when he said "yep" he would go on again. That was life, and if one questioned it, one was hit with a stick, or a boot, or a lump of rock: if one continued walking nothing happened, and that was happiness.

The Philosopher saluted this cavalcade.

"God be with you," said he.

"God and Mary be with you," said the first man.

"God, and Mary, and Patrick be with you," said the second man.

"God, and Mary, and Patrick, and Brigid be with you," said the woman.

The ass, however, did not say a thing. As the word "whoh" had not entered into the conversation he knew it was none of his business, and so he turned to the right on the new path and continued his journey.

"Where are you going to, stranger," said the first man.

"I am going to visit Angus Og," replied the Philosopher.

The man gave him a quick look.

"Well," said he, "that's the queerest story I ever heard. Listen here," he called to the others, "this man is looking for Angus Og."

The other man and woman came closer.

"What would you be wanting with Angus Og, Mister Honey?" said the woman.

"Oh," replied the Philosopher, "it's a particular thing, a family matter."

There was silence for a few minutes, and they all stepped onwards behind the ass and cart.

"How do you know where to look for himself?" said the first man again: "maybe you got the place where he lives written down in an old book or on a carved stone?"

"Or did you find the staff of Amergin or of Ossian in a bog and it written from the top to the bottom with signs?" said the second man.

"No," said the Philosopher, "it isn't that way you'd go visiting a god. What you do is, you go out from your house and walk straight away in any direction with your shadow behind you so long as it is towards a mountain, for the gods will not stay in a valley or a level plain, but only in high places; and then, if the god wants you to see him, you will go to his rath as direct as if you knew where it was, for he will be leading you with an airy thread reaching from his own place to wherever you are, and if he doesn't want to see you, you will never find out where he is, not if you were to walk for a year or twenty years."

"How do you know he wants to see you?" said the second man.

"Why wouldn't he want?" said the Philosopher.

"Maybe, Mister Honey," said the woman, "you are a holy sort of a man that a god would like well."

"Why would I be that?" said the Philosopher. "The gods like a man whether he's holy or not if he's only decent."

"Ah, well, there's plenty of that sort," said the first man. "What do you happen to have in your bag, stranger?"

"Nothing," replied the Philosopher, "but a cake and a half that was baked for my journey."

"Give me a bit of your cake, Mister Honey," said the woman. "I like to have a taste of everybody's cake."

"I will, and welcome," said the Philosopher.

"You may as well give us all a bit while you are about it," said the second man. "That woman hasn't got all the hunger of the world."

"Why not," said the Philosopher, and he divided the cake.

"There's a sup of water up yonder," said the first man, "and it will do to moisten the cake—Whoh, you devil," he roared at the ass, and the ass stood stock still on the minute.

There was a thin fringe of grass along the road near a wall, and towards this the ass began to edge very gently.

"Hike, you beast, you," shouted the man, and the ass at once hiked, but he did it in a way that brought him close to the grass. The first man took a tin can out of the cart and climbed over the little wall for water. Before he went he gave the ass three kicks on the nose, but the ass did not say a word, he only hiked still more which brought him directly on to the grass, and when the man climbed over the wall the ass commenced to crop the grass. There was a spider sitting on a hot stone in the grass. He had a small body and wide legs, and he wasn't doing anything.

"Does anybody ever kick you in the nose?" said the ass to him.

"Ay does there," said the spider; "you and your like that are always walking on me, or lying down on me, or running over me with the wheels of a cart."

"Well, why don't you stay on the wall?" said the ass.

"Sure, my wife is there," replied the spider.

"What's the harm in that?" said the ass.

"She'd eat me," said the spider, "and, anyhow, the competition on the wall is dreadful, and the flies are getting wiser and timider every season. Have you got a wife yourself, now?"

"I have not," said the ass; "I wish I had."

"You like your wife for the first while," said the spider, "and after that you hate her."

"If I had the first while I'd chance the second while," replied the ass.

"It's bachelor's talk," said the spider; "all the same, we can't keep away from them," and so saying he began to move all his legs at once in the direction of the wall. "You can only die once," said he.

"If your wife was an ass she wouldn't eat you," said the ass.

"She'd be doing something else then," replied the spider, and he climbed up the wall.

The first man came back with the can of water and they sat down on the grass and ate the cake and drank the water. All the time the woman kept her eyes fixed on the Philosopher.

"Mister Honey," said she, "I think you met us just at the right moment."

The other two men sat upright and looked at each other and then with equal intentness they looked at the woman.

"Why do you say that?" said the Philosopher.

"We were having a great argument along the road, and if we were to be talking from now to the day of doom that argument would never be finished."

"It must have been a great argument. Was it about predestination or where consciousness comes from?"

"It was not; it was which of these two men was to marry me."

"That's not a great argument," said the Philosopher.

"Isn't it," said the woman. "For seven days and six nights we didn't talk about anything else, and that's a great argument or I'd like to know what is."

"But where is the trouble, ma'am?" said the Philosopher.

"It's this," she replied, "that I can't make up my mind which of the men I'll take, for I like one as well as the other and better, and I'd as soon have one as the other and rather."

"It's a hard case," said the Philosopher.

"It is," said the woman, "and I'm sick and sorry with the trouble of it."

"And why did you say that I had come up in a good minute?"

"Because, Mister Honey, when a woman has two men to choose from she doesn't know what to do, for two men always become like brothers so that you wouldn't know which of them was which: there isn't any more difference between two men than there is between a couple of hares. But when there's three men to choose from, there's no trouble at all; and so I say that it's yourself I'll marry this night and no one else— and let you two men be sitting quiet in your places, for I'm telling you what I'll do and that's the end of it."

JAMES STEPHENS

"I'll give you my word," said the first man, "that I'm just as glad as you are to have it over and done with."

"Moidered I was," said the second man, "with the whole argument, and the this and that of it, and you not able to say a word but—maybe I will and maybe I won't, and this is true and that is true, and why not to me and why not to him—I'll get a sleep this night."

The Philosopher was perplexed.

"You cannot marry me, ma'am," said he, "because I'm married already."

The woman turned round on him angrily.

"Don't be making any argument with me now," said she, "for I won't stand it."

The first man looked fiercely at the Philosopher, and then motioned to his companion.

"Give that man a clout in the jaw," said he.

The second man was preparing to do this when the woman intervened angrily.

"Keep your hands to yourself," said she, "or it'll be the worse for you. I'm well able to take care of my own husband," and she drew nearer and sat between the Philosopher and the men.

At that moment the Philosopher's cake lost all its savour, and he packed the remnant into his wallet. They all sat silently looking at their feet and thinking each one according to his nature. The Philosopher's mind, which for the past day had been in eclipse, stirred faintly to meet these new circumstances, but without much result. There was a flutter at his heart which was terrifying, but not unpleasant. Quickening through his apprehension was an expectancy which stirred his pulses into speed. So rapidly did his blood flow, so quickly were an hundred impressions visualized and recorded, so violent was the surface movement of his brain that he did not realize he was unable to think and that he was only seeing and feeling.

The first man stood up.

"The night will be coming on soon," said he, "and we had better be walking on if we want to get a good place to sleep. Yep, you devil," he roared at the ass, and the ass began to move almost before he lifted his head from the grass. The two men walked one on either side of the cart, and the woman and the Philosopher walked behind at the tail-board.

"If you were feeling tired, or anything like that, Mister Honey," said the woman, "you could climb up into the little cart, and nobody would say a word to you, for I can see that you are not used to travelling."

"I am not indeed, ma'am," he replied; "this is the first time I ever came on a journey, and if it wasn't for Angus Og I wouldn't put a foot out of my own place for ever."

"Put Angus Og out of your head, my dear," she replied, "for what would the likes of you and me be saying to a god. He might put a curse on us would sink us into the ground or burn us up like a grip of straw. Be contented now, I'm saying, for if there is a woman in the world who knows all things I am that woman myself, and if you tell your trouble to me I'll tell you the thing to do just as good as Angus himself, and better perhaps."

"That is very interesting," said the Philosopher. "What kind of things do you know best?"

"If you were to ask one of them two men walking beside the ass they'd tell you plenty of things they saw me do when they could do nothing themselves. When there wasn't a road to take anywhere I showed them a road, and when there wasn't a bit of food in the world I gave them food, and when they were bet to the last I put shillings in their hands, and that's the reason they wanted to marry me."

"Do you call that kind of thing wisdom?" said the Philosopher.

"Why wouldn't I?" said she. "Isn't it wisdom to go through the world without fear and not to be hungry in a hungry hour?"

"I suppose it is," he replied, "but I never thought of it that way myself."

"And what would you call wisdom?"

"I couldn't rightly say now," he replied, "but I think it was not to mind about the world, and not to care whether you were hungry or not, and not to live in the world at all but only in your own head, for the world is a tyrannous place. You have to raise yourself above things instead of letting things raise themselves above you. We must not be slaves to each other, and we must not be slaves to our necessities either. That is the problem of existence. There is no dignity in life at all if hunger can shout 'stop' at every turn of the road and the day's journey is measured by the distance between one sleep and the next sleep. Life is all slavery, and Nature is driving us with the whips of appetite and weariness; but when a slave rebels he ceases to be a slave, and when we are too hungry to live we can die and have our laugh. I believe that Nature is just as alive as we are, and that she is as much frightened of us as we are of her, and, mind you this, mankind has declared war against Nature and we will win. She does not understand yet that her geologic periods won't do any longer, and that while she is pattering along the line of least resistance we are going to travel fast and far until we find her, and then, being a female, she is bound to give in when she is challenged."

"It's good talk," said the woman, "but it's foolishness. Women never give in unless they get what they want, and where's the harm to them then? You have to live in the world, my dear, whether you like it or not, and, believe me now, that there isn't any wisdom but to keep clear of the hunger, for if that gets near enough it will make a hare of you. Sure, listen to reason now like a good man. What is Nature at all but a word that learned men have made to talk about. There's clay and gods and men, and they are good friends enough."

The sun had long since gone down, and the grey evening was bowing over the land, hiding the mountain peaks, and putting a shadow round the scattered bushes and the wide clumps of heather.

"I know a place up here where we can stop for the night," said she, "and there's a little shebeen round the bend of the road where we can get anything we want."

At the word "whoh" the ass stopped and one of the men took the harness off him. When he was unyoked the man gave him two kicks: "Be off with you, you devil, and see if you can get anything to eat," he roared. The ass trotted a few paces off and searched about until he found some grass. He ate this, and when he had eaten as much as he wanted he returned and lay down under a wall. He lay for a long time looking in the one direction, and at last he put his head down and went to sleep. While he was sleeping he kept one ear up and the other ear down for about twenty minutes, and then he put the first ear down and the other one up, and he kept on doing this all the night. If he had anything to lose you wouldn't mind him setting up sentries, but he hadn't a thing in the world except his skin and his bones, and no one would be bothered stealing them.

One of the men took a long bottle out of the cart and walked up the road with it. The other man lifted out a tin bucket which was punched all over with jagged holes. Then he took out some sods of turf and lumps of wood and he put these in the bucket, and in a few minutes he had a very nice fire lit. A pot of water was put on to boil, and the woman cut up a great lump of bacon which she put into the pot. She had eight eggs in a place in the cart, and a flat loaf of bread, and some cold boiled potatoes, and she spread her apron on the ground and arranged these things on it.

The other man came down the road again with his big bottle filled with porter, and he put this in a safe place. Then they emptied everything out of the cart and hoisted it over the little wall. They turned the cart on one side and pulled it near to the fire, and they all sat inside the cart and ate their supper. When supper was done they lit their pipes, and the woman lit a pipe also. The bottle of porter was brought forward, and they took drinks in turn out of the bottle, and smoked their pipes, and talked.

There was no moon that night, and no stars, so that just beyond the fire there was a thick darkness which one would not like to look at, it was so cold and empty. While talking they all kept their eyes fixed on the red fire, or watched the smoke from their pipes drifting and curling away against the blackness, and disappearing as suddenly as lightning.

"I wonder," said the first man, "what it was gave you the idea of marrying this man instead of myself or my comrade, for we are young, hardy men, and he is getting old, God help him!"

"Aye, indeed," said the second man; "he's as grey as a badger, and there's no flesh on his bones."

"You have a right to ask that," said she, "and I'll tell you why I didn't marry either of you. You are only a pair of tinkers going from one place to another, and not knowing anything at all of fine things; but himself was walking along the road looking for strange, high adventures, and it's a man like that a woman would be wishing to marry if he was twice as old as he is. When did either of you go out in the daylight looking for a god and you not caring what might happen to you or where you went?"

"What I'm thinking," said the second man, "is that if you leave the gods alone they'll leave you alone. It's no trouble to them to do whatever is right themselves, and what call would men like us have to go mixing or meddling with their high affairs?"

"I thought all along that you were a timid man," said she, "and now I know it." She turned again to the Philosopher—"Take off your boots, Mister Honey, the way you'll rest easy, and I'll be making down a soft bed for you in the cart."

In order to take off his boots the Philosopher had to stand up, for in the cart they were too cramped for freedom. He moved backwards a space from the fire and took off his boots. He could see the woman stretching sacks and clothes inside the cart, and the two men smoking quietly and handing the big bottle from one to the other. Then in his stockinged feet he stepped a little farther from the fire, and, after another look, he turned and walked quietly away into the blackness. In a few minutes he heard a shout from behind him, and then a number of shouts and then these died away into a plaintive murmur of voices, and next he was alone in the greatest darkness he had ever known.

He put on his boots and walked onwards. He had no idea where the road lay, and every moment he stumbled into a patch of heather or prickly furze. The ground was very uneven with unexpected mounds and deep hollows: here and there were water-soaked, soggy places, and into these cold ruins he sank ankle deep. There was no longer an earth or a sky, but only a black void and a thin wind and a fierce silence which seemed to listen to him as he went. Out of that silence a thundering laugh might boom at an instant and stop again while he stood appalled in the blind vacancy.

The hill began to grow more steep and rocks were lying everywhere in his path. He could not see an inch in front, and so he went with his hands out-stretched like a blind man who stumbles painfully along. After a time he was nearly worn out with cold and weariness, but he dared not sit down anywhere; the darkness was so intense that it frightened him, and the overwhelming, crafty silence frightened him also.

At last, and at a great distance, he saw a flickering, waving light, and he went towards this through drifts of heather, and over piled rocks and sodden bogland. When he came to the light he saw it was a torch of thick branches, the flame whereof blew hither and thither on the wind. The torch was fastened against a great cliff of granite by an iron band. At one side there was a dark opening in the rock, so he said: "I will go in there and sleep until the morning comes," and he went in. At a very short distance the cleft turned again to the right, and here there was another torch fixed. When he turned this corner he stood for an instant in speechless astonishment, and then he covered his face and bowed down upon the ground.

BOOK 3
THE TWO GODS

Chapter 12

Caitilin Ni Murrachu was sitting alone in the little cave behind Gort na Cloca Mora. Her companion had gone out as was his custom to walk in the sunny morning and to sound his pipe in desolate, green spaces whence, perhaps, the wanderer of his desire might hear the guiding sweetness. As she sat she was thinking. The last few days had awakened her body, and had also awakened her mind, for with the one awakening comes the other. The despondency which had touched her previously when tending her father's cattle came to her again, but recognizably now. She knew the thing which the wind had whispered in the sloping field and for which she had no name—it was Happiness. Faintly she shadowed it forth, but yet she could not see it. It was only a pearl-pale wraith, almost formless, too tenuous to be touched by her hands, and too aloof to be spoken to. Pan had told her that he was the giver of happiness, but he had given her only unrest and fever and a longing which could not be satisfied. Again there was a want, and she could not formulate, or even realize it with any closeness. Her new-born Thought had promised everything, even as Pan, and it had given—she could not say that it had given her nothing or anything. Its limits were too quickly divinable. She had found the Tree of Knowledge, but about on every side a great wall soared blackly enclosing her in from the Tree of Life—a wall which her thought was unable to surmount even while instinct urged that it must topple before her advance; but instinct may not advance when thought has schooled it in the science of unbelief; and this wall will not be conquered until Thought and Instinct are wed, and the first son of that bridal will be called The Scaler of the Wall.

So, after the quiet weariness of ignorance, the unquiet weariness of thought had fallen upon her. That travail of mind which, through countless generations, has throed to the birth of an ecstasy, the prophecy which humanity has sworn must be fulfilled, seeing through whatever mists and doubtings the vision of a gaiety wherein the innocence of the morning will not any longer be strange to our maturity.

While she was so thinking Pan returned, a little disheartened that he had found no person to listen to his pipings. He had been seated but a little time when suddenly, from without, a chorus of birds burst into joyous singing. Limpid and liquid cadenzas, mellow flutings, and the sweet treble of infancy met and danced and piped in the airy soundings.

A round, soft tenderness of song rose and fell, broadened and soared, and then the high flight was snatched, eddied a moment, and was borne away to a more slender and wonderful loftiness, until, from afar, that thrilling song turned on the very apex of sweetness, dipped steeply and flashed its joyous return to the exultations of its mates below, rolling an ecstasy of song which for one moment gladdened the whole world and the sad people who moved thereon; then the singing ceased as suddenly as it began, a swift shadow darkened the passage, and Angus Og came into the cave.

Caitilin sprang from her seat Frighted, and Pan also made a half movement towards rising, but instantly sank back again to his negligent, easy posture.

The god was slender and as swift as a wind. His hair swung about his face like golden blossoms. His eyes were mild and dancing and his lips smiled with quiet sweetness. About his head there flew perpetually a ring of singing birds, and when he spoke his voice came sweetly from a centre of sweetness.

"Health to you, daughter of Murrachu," said he, and he sat down.

"I do not know you, sir," the terrified girl whispered.

"I cannot be known until I make myself known," he replied. "I am called Infinite Joy, O daughter of Murrachu, and I am called Love."

The girl gazed doubtfully from one to the other.

Pan looked up from his pipes.

"I also am called Love," said he gently, "and I am called Joy."

Angus Og looked for the first time at Pan.

"Singer of the Vine," said he, "I know your names—they are Desire and Fever and Lust and Death. Why have you come from your own place to spy upon my pastures and my quiet fields?"

Pan replied mildly.

"The mortal gods move by the Immortal Will, and, therefore, I am here."

"And I am here," said Angus.

"Give me a sign," said Pan, "that I must go."

Angus Og lifted his hand and from without there came again the triumphant music of the birds.

"It is a sign," said he, "the voice of Dana speaking in the air," and, saying so, he made obeisance to the great mother.

Pan lifted his hand, and from afar there came the lowing of the cattle and the thin voices of the goats.

"It is a sign," said he, "the voice of Demeter speaking from the earth," and he also bowed deeply to the mother of the world.

Again Angus Og lifted his hand, and in it there appeared a spear, bright and very terrible.

But Pan only said, "Can a spear divine the Eternal Will?" and Angus Og put his weapon aside, and he said: "The girl will choose between us, for the Divine Mood shines in the heart of man."

Then Caitilin Ni Murrachu came forward and sat between the gods, but Pan stretched out his hand and drew her to him, so that she sat resting against his shoulder and his arm was about her body.

"We will speak the truth to this girl," said Angus Og.

"Can the gods speak otherwise?" said Pan, and he laughed with delight.

"It is the difference between us," replied Angus Og. "She will judge."

"Shepherd Girl," said Pan, pressing her with his arm, "you will judge between us. Do you know what is the greatest thing in the world?—because it is of that you will have to judge."

"I have heard," the girl replied, "two things called the greatest things. You," she continued to Pan, "said it was Hunger, and long ago my father said that Commonsense was the greatest thing in the world."

"I have not told you," said Angus Og, "what I consider is the greatest thing in the world."

"It is your right to speak," said Pan.

"The greatest thing in the world," said Angus Og, "is the Divine Imagination."

"Now," said Pan, "we know all the greatest things and we can talk of them."

"The daughter of Murrachu," continued Angus Og, "has told us what you think and what her father thinks, but she has not told us what she thinks herself. Tell us, Caitilin Ni Murrachu, what you think is the greatest thing in the world."

So Caitilin Ni Murrachu thought for a few moments and then replied timidly.

"I think that Happiness is the greatest thing in the world," said she.

Hearing this they sat in silence for a little time, and then Angus Og spoke again "The Divine Imagination may only be known through the thoughts of His creatures. A man has said Commonsense and a woman has said Happiness are the greatest things in the world. These things are male and female, for Commonsense is Thought and Happiness is

Emotion, and until they embrace in Love the will of Immensity cannot be fruitful. For, behold, there has been no marriage of humanity since time began. Men have but coupled with their own shadows. The desire that sprang from their heads they pursued, and no man has yet known the love of a woman. And women have mated with the shadows of their own hearts, thinking fondly that the arms of men were about them. I saw my son dancing with an Idea, and I said to him, 'With what do you dance, my son?' and he replied, 'I make merry with the wife of my affection,' and truly she was shaped as a woman is shaped, but it was an Idea he danced with and not a woman. And presently he went away to his labours, and then his Idea arose and her humanity came upon her so that she was clothed with beauty and terror, and she went apart and danced with the servant of my son, and there was great joy of that dancing—for a person in the wrong place is an Idea and not a person. Man is Thought and woman is Intuition, and they have never mated. There is a gulf between them and it is called Fear, and what they fear is, that their strengths shall be taken from them and they may no longer be tyrants. The Eternal has made love blind, for it is not by science, but by intuition alone, that he may come to his beloved; but desire, which is science, has many eyes and sees so vastly that he passes his love in the press, saying there is no love, and he propagates miserably on his own delusions. The finger-tips are guided by God, but the devil looks through the eyes of all creatures so that they may wander in the errors of reason and justify themselves of their wanderings. The desire of a man shall be Beauty, but he has fashioned a slave in his mind and called it Virtue. The desire of a woman shall be Wisdom, but she has formed a beast in her blood and called it Courage: but the real virtue is courage, and the real courage is liberty, and the real liberty is wisdom, and Wisdom is the son of Thought and Intuition; and his names also are Innocence and Adoration and Happiness."

When Angus Og had said these words he ceased, and for a time there was silence in the little cave. Caitilin had covered her face with her hands and would not look at him, but Pan drew the girl closer to his side and peered sideways, laughing at Angus.

"Has the time yet come for the girl to judge between us?" said he.

"Daughter of Murrachu," said Angus Og, "will you come away with me from this place?"

Caitilin then looked at the god in great distress. "I do not know what to do," said she. "Why do you both want me? I have given myself to Pan, and his arms are about me."

"I want you," said Angus Og, "because the world has forgotten me. In all my nation there is no remembrance of me. I, wandering on the hills of my country, am lonely indeed. I am the desolate god forbidden to utter my happy laughter. I hide the silver of my speech and the gold of my merriment. I live in the holes of the rocks and the dark caves of the sea. I weep in the morning because I may not laugh, and in the evening I go abroad and am not happy. Where I have kissed a bird has flown; where I have trod a flower has sprung. But Thought has snared my birds in his nets and sold them in the market-places. Who will deliver me from Thought, from the base holiness of Intellect, the maker of chains and traps? Who will save me from the holy impurity of Emotion, whose daughters are Envy and Jealousy and Hatred, who plucks my flowers to ornament her lusts and my little leaves to shrivel on the breasts of infamy? Lo, I am sealed in the caves of nonentity until the head and the heart shall come together in fruitfulness, until Thought has wept for Love, and Emotion has purified herself to meet her lover. Tirna-nog is the heart of a man and the head of a woman. Widely they are separated. Self-centred they stand, and between them the seas of space are flooding desolately. No voice can shout across those shores. No eye can bridge them, nor any desire bring them together until the blind god shall find them on the wavering stream—not as an arrow searches straightly from a bow, but gently, imperceptibly as a feather on the wind reaches the ground on a hundred starts; not with the compass and the chart, but by the breath of the Almighty which blows from all quarters without care and without ceasing. Night and day it urges from the outside to the inside. It gathers ever to the centre. From the far without to the deep within, trembling from the body to the soul until the head of a woman and the heart of a man are filled with the Divine Imagination. Hymen, Hymenaea! I sing to the ears that are stopped, the eyes that are sealed, and the minds that do not labour. Sweetly I sing on the hillside. The blind shall look within and not without; the deaf shall hearken to the murmur of their own veins, and be enchanted with the wisdom of sweetness; the thoughtless shall think without effort as the lightning flashes, that the hand of Innocence may reach to the stars, that the feet of Adoration may dance to the Father of Joy, and the laugh of Happiness be answered by the Voice of Benediction."

Thus Angus Og sang in the cave, and ere he had ceased Caitilin Ni Murrachu withdrew herself from the arms of her desires. But so strong was the hold of Pan upon her that when she was free her body bore the marks of his grip, and many days passed away before these marks faded.

Then Pan arose in silence, taking his double reed in his hand, and the girl wept, beseeching him to stay to be her brother and the brother of her beloved, but Pan smiled and said: "Your beloved is my father and my son. He is yesterday and to-morrow. He is the nether and the upper millstone, and I am crushed between until I kneel again before the throne from whence I came," and, saying so, he embraced Angus Og most tenderly and went his way to the quiet fields, and across the slopes of the mountains, and beyond the blue distances of space.

And in a little time Caitilin Ni Murrachu went with her companion across the brow of the hill, and she did not go with him because she had understood his words, nor because he was naked and unashamed, but only because his need of her was very great, and, therefore, she loved him, and stayed his feet in the way, and was concerned lest he should stumble.

BOOK 4
THE PHILOSOPHER'S RETURN

Chapter 13

Which is, the Earth or the creatures that move upon it, the more important? This is a question prompted solely by intellectual arrogance, for in life there is no greater and no less. The thing that is has justified its own importance by mere existence, for that is the great and equal achievement. If life were arranged for us from without such a question of supremacy would assume importance, but life is always from within, and is modified or extended by our own appetites, aspirations, and central activities. From without we get pollen and the refreshment of space and quietude—it is sufficient. We might ask, is the Earth anything more than an extension of our human consciousness, or are we, moving creatures, only projections of the Earth's antennae? But these matters have no value save as a field wherein Thought, like a wise lamb, may frolic merrily. And all would be very well if Thought would but continue to frolic, instead of setting up first as locum tenens for Intuition and sticking to the job, and afterwards as the counsel and critic of Omnipotence. Everything has two names, and everything is twofold. The name of male Thought as it faces the world is Philosophy, but the name it bears in Tirna-nog is Delusion. Female Thought is called Socialism on earth, but in Eternity it is known as Illusion; and this is so because there has been no matrimony of minds, but only an hermaphroditic propagation of automatic ideas, which in their due rotation assume dominance and reign severely. To the world this system of thought, because it is consecutive, is known as Logic, but Eternity has written it down in the Book of Errors as Mechanism: for life may not be consecutive, but explosive and variable, else it is a shackled and timorous slave.

One of the great troubles of life is that Reason has taken charge of the administration of Justice, and by mere identification it has achieved the crown and sceptre of its master. But the imperceptible usurpation was recorded, and discriminating minds understand the chasm which still divides the pretender Law from the exiled King. In a like manner, and with feigned humility, the Cold Demon advanced to serve Religion, and by guile and violence usurped her throne; but the pure in heart still fly from the spectre Theology to dance in ecstasy before the starry and eternal goddess. Statecraft, also, that tender Shepherd of the Flocks, has been despoiled of his crook and bell, and wanders in unknown desolation while, beneath the banner of Politics, Reason sits howling over an intellectual chaos.

Justice is the maintaining of equilibrium. The blood of Cain must cry, not from the lips of the Avenger, but from the aggrieved Earth herself who demands that atonement shall be made for a disturbance of her consciousness. All justice is, therefore, readjustment. A thwarted consciousness has every right to clamour for assistance, but not for punishment. This latter can only be sought by timorous and egotistic Intellect, which sees the Earth from which it has emerged and into which it must return again in its own despite, and so, being self-centred and envious and a renegade from life, Reason is more cruelly unjust, and more timorous than any other manifestation of the divinely erratic energy—erratic, because, as has been said, "the crooked roads are the roads of genius." Nature grants to all her creatures an unrestricted liberty, quickened by competitive appetite, to succeed or to fail; save only to Reason, her Demon of Order, which can do neither, and whose wings she has clipped for some reason with which I am not yet acquainted. It may be that an unrestricted mentality would endanger her own intuitive perceptions by shackling all her other organs of perception, or annoy her by vexatious efforts at creative rivalry.

It will, therefore, be understood that when the Leprecauns of Gort na Cloca Mora acted in the manner about to be recorded, they were not prompted by any lewd passion for revenge, but were merely striving to reconstruct a rhythm which was their very existence, and which must have been of direct importance to the Earth. Revenge is the vilest passion known to life. It has made Law possible, and by doing so it gave to Intellect the first grip at that universal dominion which is its ambition. A Leprecaun is of more value to the Earth than is a Prime Minister or a stockbroker, because a Leprecaun dances and makes merry, while a Prime Minister knows nothing of these natural virtues—consequently, an injury done to a Leprecaun afflicts the Earth with misery, and justice is, for these reasons, an imperative and momentous necessity.

A community of Leprecauns without a crock of gold is a blighted and merriless community, and they are certainly justified in seeking sympathy and assistance for the recovery of so essential a treasure. But the steps whereby the Leprecauns of Gort na Cloca Mora sought to regain their property must for ever brand their memory with a certain odium. It should be remembered in their favour that they were cunningly and cruelly encompassed. Not only was their gold stolen, but it was buried in such a position as placed it under the protection of their own communal honour, and the household of their enemy was secured against their active and righteous malice, because the Thin Woman of Inis Magrath belonged to the most powerful Shee of Ireland. It is in circumstances such as these that dangerous alliances are made, and, for the first time in history, the elemental beings invoked bourgeois assistance.

They were loath to do it, and justice must record the fact. They were angry when they did it, and anger is both mental and intuitive blindness. It is not the beneficent blindness which prevents one from seeing without, but it is that desperate darkness which cloaks the within, and hides the heart and the brain from each other's husbandry and wifely recognition. But even those mitigating circumstances cannot justify the course they adopted, and the wider idea must be sought for, that out of evil good must ultimately come, or else evil is vitiated beyond even the redemption of usage. When they were able to realize of what they had been guilty, they were very sorry indeed, and endeavoured to publish their repentance in many ways; but, lacking atonement, repentance is only a post-mortem virtue which is good for nothing but burial.

When the Leprecauns of Gort na Cloca Mora found they were unable to regain their crock of gold by any means they laid an anonymous information at the nearest Police Station showing that two dead bodies would be found under the hearthstone in the hut of Coille Doraca, and the inference to be drawn from their crafty missive was that these bodies had been murdered by the Philosopher for reasons very discreditable to him.

The Philosopher had been scarcely more than three hours on his journey to Angus Og when four policemen approached the little house from as many different directions, and without any trouble they effected an entrance. The Thin Woman of Inis Magrath and the two children heard from afar their badly muffled advance, and on discovering the character of their visitors they concealed themselves among the thickly clustering trees. Shortly after the men had entered the hut loud and sustained noises began to issue therefrom, and in about twenty minutes the invaders emerged again bearing the bodies of the Grey Woman of Dun Gortin and her husband. They wrenched the door off its hinges, and, placing the bodies on the door, proceeded at a rapid pace through the trees and disappeared in a short time. When they had departed the Thin Woman and the children returned to their home and over the yawning hearth the Thin Woman pronounced a long and fervid malediction wherein policemen were exhibited naked before the blushes of Eternity. . .

With your good-will let us now return to the Philosopher.

Following his interview with Angus Og the Philosopher received the blessing of the god and returned on his homeward journey. When he left the cave he had no knowledge where he was nor whether he should turn to the right hand or to the left. This alone was his guiding idea, that as he had come up the mountain on his first journey his home-going must, by mere opposition, be down the mountain, and, accordingly, he set his face downhill and trod lustily forward. He had stamped up the hill with vigour, he strode down it in ecstasy. He tossed his voice on every wind that went by. From the wells of forgetfulness he regained the shining words and gay melodies which his childhood had delighted in, and these he sang loudly and unceasingly as he marched. The sun had not yet risen but, far away, a quiet brightness was creeping over the sky. The daylight, however, was near the full, one slender veil only remaining of the shadows, and a calm, unmoving quietude brooded from the grey sky to the whispering earth. The birds had begun to bestir themselves but not to sing. Now and again a solitary wing feathered the chill air; but for the most part the birds huddled closer in the swinging nests, or under the bracken, or in the tufty grass. Here a faint twitter was heard and ceased. A little farther a drowsy voice called "cheep-cheep" and turned again to the warmth of its wing. The very grasshoppers were silent. The creatures who range in the night time had returned to their cells and were setting their households in order, and those who belonged to the day hugged their comfort for but one minute longer. Then the first level beam stepped like a mild angel to the mountain top. The slender radiance brightened and grew strong. The grey veil faded away. The birds leaped from their nests. The grasshoppers awakened and were busy at a stroke. Voice called to voice without ceasing, and, momently, a song thrilled for a few wide seconds. But for the most part it was chatter-chatter they went as they soared and plunged and swept, each bird eager for its breakfast.

The Philosopher thrust his hand into his wallet and found there the last broken remnants of his cake, and the instant his hand touched the food he was seized by a hunger so furious that he sat down where he stopped and prepared to eat.

The place where he sat was a raised bank under a hedge, and this place directly fronted a clumsy wooden gate leading into a great field. When the Philosopher had seated himself he raised his eyes and saw through the gate a small company approaching. There were four men and three women, and each of them carried a metal pail. The Philosopher with a sigh returned the cake to his wallet, saying:

"All men are brothers, and it may be that these people are as hungry as I am."

In a short time the strangers came near. The foremost of them was a huge man who was bearded to the eyelids and who moved like a strong wind. He opened the gate by removing a piece of wood wherewith it was jammed, and he and his companions passed through, whereupon he closed the gate and secured it. To this man, as being the eldest, the Philosopher approached.

"I am about to breakfast," said he, "and if you are hungry perhaps you would like to eat with me."

"Why not," said the man, "for the person who would refuse a kind invitation is a dog. These are my three sons and three of my daughters, and we are all thankful to you."

Saying this he sat down on the bank and his companions, placing their pails behind them, did likewise. The Philosopher divided his cake into eight pieces and gave one to each person.

"I am sorry it is so little," said he.

"A gift," said the bearded man, "is never little," and he courteously ate his piece in three bites although he could have easily eaten it in one, and his children also.

"That was a good, satisfying cake," said he when he had finished; "it was well baked and well shared, but," he continued, "I am in a difficulty and maybe you could advise me what to do, sir?"

"What might be your trouble?" said the Philosopher.

"It is this," said the man. "Every morning when we go out to milk the cows the mother of my clann gives to each of us a parcel of food so that we need not be any hungrier than we like; but now we have had a good breakfast with you, what shall we do with the food that we brought with us? The woman of the house would not be pleased if we carried it back to her, and if we threw food away it would be a sin. If it was not disrespectful to your breakfast the boys and girls here might be able to get rid of it by eating it, for, as you know, young people can always eat a bit more, no matter how much they have already eaten."

"It would surely be better to eat it than to waste it," said the Philosopher wistfully.

The young people produced large parcels of food from their pockets and opened them, and the bearded man said, "I have a little one myself also, and it would not be wasted if you were kind enough to help me to eat it," and he pulled out his parcel, which was twice as big as any of the others.

He opened the parcel and handed the larger part of its contents to the Philosopher; he then plunged a tin vessel into one of the milk pails and set this also by the Philosopher, and, instantly, they all began to eat with furious appetite.

When the meal was finished the Philosopher filled his tobacco pipe and the bearded man and his three sons did likewise.

"Sir," said the bearded man, "I would be glad to know why you are travelling abroad so early in the morning, for, at this hour, no one stirs but the sun and the birds and the folk who, like ourselves, follow the cattle?"

"I will tell you that gladly," said the Philosopher, "if you will tell me your name."

"My name," said the bearded man, "is Mac Cul."

"Last night," said the Philosopher, "when I came from the house of Angus Og in the Caves of the Sleepers of Erinn I was bidden say to a man named Mac Cul—that the horses had trampled in their sleep and the sleepers had turned on their sides."

"Sir," said the bearded man, "your words thrill in my heart like music, but my head does not understand them."

"I have learned," said the Philosopher, "that the head does not hear anything until the heart has listened, and that what the heart knows to-day the head will understand to-morrow."

"All the birds of the world are singing in my soul," said the bearded man, "and I bless you because you have filled me with hope and pride."

So the Philosopher shook him by the hand, and he shook the hands of his sons and daughters who bowed before him at the mild command of their father, and when he had gone a little way he looked around again and he saw that group of people standing where he had left them, and the bearded man was embracing his children on the highroad.

A bend in the path soon shut them from view, and then the Philosopher, fortified by food and the freshness of the morning, strode onwards singing for very joy. It was still early, but now the birds had eaten their breakfasts and were devoting themselves to each other. They rested side by side on the branches of the trees and on the hedges, they danced in the air in happy brotherhoods and they sang to one another amiable and pleasant ditties.

When the Philosopher had walked for a long time he felt a little weary and sat down to refresh himself in the shadow of a great tree. Hard by there was a house of rugged stone. Long years ago it had been a castle, and, even now, though patched by time and misfortune its front was warlike and frowning. While he sat a young woman came along the road and stood gazing earnestly at this house. Her hair was as black as night and as smooth as still water, but her face came so stormily forward that her quiet attitude had yet no quietness in it. To her, after a few moments, the Philosopher spoke.

"Girl," said he, "why do you look so earnestly at the house?"

The girl turned her pale face and stared at him.

"I did not notice you sitting under the tree," said she, and she came slowly forward.

"Sit down by me," said the Philosopher, "and we will talk. If you are in any trouble tell it to me, and perhaps you will talk the heaviest part away."

"I will sit beside you willingly," said the girl, and she did so.

"It is good to talk trouble over," he continued. "Do you know that talk is a real thing? There is more power in speech than many people conceive. Thoughts come from God, they are born through the marriage of the head and the lungs. The head moulds the thought into the form of words, then it is borne and sounded on the air which has been already in the secret kingdoms of the body, which goes in bearing life and come out freighted with wisdom. For this reason a lie is very terrible, because it is turning mighty and incomprehensible things to base uses, and is burdening the life-giving element with a foul return for its goodness; but those who speak the truth and whose words are the symbols of wisdom and beauty, these purify the whole world and daunt contagion. The only trouble the body can know is disease. All other miseries come from the brain, and, as these belong to thought, they can be driven out by their master as unruly and unpleasant vagabonds; for a mental trouble should be spoken to, confronted, reprimanded and so dismissed. The brain cannot afford to harbour any but pleasant and eager citizens who will do their part in making laughter and holiness for the world, for that is the duty of thought."

While the Philosopher spoke the girl had been regarding him steadfastly.

"Sir," said she, "we tell our hearts to a young man and our heads to an old man, and when the heart is a fool the head is bound to be a liar. I can tell you the things I know, but how will I tell you the things I feel when I myself do not understand them? If I say these words to you 'I love a man' I do not say anything at all, and you do not hear one of the words which my heart is repeating over and over to itself in the silence of my body. Young people are fools in their heads and old people are fools in their hearts, and they can only look at each other and pass by in wonder."

"You are wrong," said the Philosopher. "An old person can take your hand like this and say, 'May every good thing come to you, my daughter.' For all trouble there is sympathy, and for love there is memory, and these are the head and the heart talking to each other in quiet friendship. What the heart knows to-day the head will understand to-morrow, and as the head must be the scholar of the heart it is necessary that our hearts be purified and free from every false thing, else we are tainted beyond personal redemption."

"Sir," said the girl, "I know of two great follies—they are love and speech, for when these are given they can never be taken back again, and the person to whom these are given is not any richer, but the giver is made poor and abashed. I gave my love to a man who did not want it. I told him of my love, and he lifted his eyelids at me; that is my trouble."

For a moment the Philosopher sat in stricken silence looking on the ground. He had a strange disinclination to look at the girl although he felt her eyes fixed steadily on him. But in a little while he did look at her and spoke again.

"To carry gifts to an ungrateful person cannot be justified and need not be mourned for. If your love is noble why do you treat it meanly? If it is lewd the man was right to reject it."

"We love as the wind blows," she replied.

"There is a thing," said the Philosopher, "and it is both the biggest and the littlest thing in the world."

"What is that?" said the girl.

"It is pride," he answered. "It lives in an empty house. The head which has never been visited by the heart is the house pride lives in. You are in error, my dear, and not in love. Drive out the knave pride, put a flower in your hair and walk freely again."

The girl laughed, and suddenly her pale face became rosy as the dawn and as radiant and lovely as a cloud. She shed warmth and beauty about her as she leaned forward.

"You are wrong," she whispered, "because he does love me; but he does not know it yet. He is young and full of fury, and has no time to look at women, but he looked at me. My heart knows it and my head knows it, but I am impatient and yearn for him to look at me again. His heart will remember me to-morrow, and he will come searching for me with prayers and tears, with shouts and threats. I will be very hard to find to-morrow when he holds out his arms to the air and the sky, and is astonished and frightened to find me nowhere. I will hide from him to-morrow, and frown at him when he speaks, and turn aside when he follows me: until the day after to-morrow when he will frighten me with his anger, and hold me with his furious hands, and make me look at him."

Saying this the girl arose and prepared to go away.

"He is in that house," said she, "and I would not let him see me here for anything in the world."

"You have wasted all my time," said the Philosopher, smiling.

"What else is time for?" said the girl, and she kissed the Philosopher and ran swiftly down the road.

She had been gone but a few moments when a man came out of the grey house and walked quickly across the grass. When he reached the hedge separating the field from the road he tossed his two arms in the air, swung them down, and jumped over the hedge into the roadway. He was a short, dark youth, and so swift and sudden were his movements that he seemed to look on every side at the one moment although he bore furiously to his own direction.

The Philosopher addressed him mildly.

"That was a good jump," said he.

The young man spun around from where he stood, and was by the Philosopher's side in an instant.

"It would be a good jump for other men," said he, "but it is only a little jump for me. You are very dusty, sir; you must have travelled a long distance to-day."

"A long distance," replied the Philosopher. "Sit down here, my friend, and keep me company for a little time."

"I do not like sitting down," said the young man, "but I always consent to a request, and I always accept friendship." And, so saying, he threw himself down on the grass.

"Do you work in that big house?" said the Philosopher.

"I do," he replied. "I train the hounds for a fat, jovial man, full of laughter and insolence."

"I think you do not like your master."

"Believe, sir, that I do not like any master; but this man I hate. I have been a week in his service, and he has not once looked on me as on a friend. This very day, in the kennel, he passed me as though I were a tree or a stone. I almost leaped to catch him by the throat and say: 'Dog, do you not salute your fellow-man?' But I looked after him and let him go, for it would be an unpleasant thing to strangle a fat person."

"If you are displeased with your master should you not look for another occupation?" said the Philosopher.

"I was thinking of that, and I was thinking whether I ought to kill him or marry his daughter. She would have passed me by as her father did, but I would not let a woman do that to me: no man would."

"What did you do to her?" said the Philosopher.

The young man chuckled "I did not look at her the first time, and when she came near me the second time I looked another way, and on the third day she spoke to me, and while she stood I looked over her shoulder distantly. She said she hoped I would be happy in my new home, and she made her voice sound pleasant while she said it; but I thanked her and turned away carelessly."

"Is the girl beautiful?" said the Philosopher.

"I do not know," he replied; "I have not looked at her yet, although now I see her everywhere. I think she is a woman who would annoy me if I married her."

"If you haven't seen her, how can you think that?"

"She has tame feet," said the youth. "I looked at them and they got frightened. Where have you travelled from, sir?"

"I will tell you that," said the Philosopher, "if you will tell me your name."

"It is easily told," he answered; "my name is MacCulain."

"When I came last night," said the Philosopher, "from the place of Angus Og in the cave of the Sleepers of Erinn I was bidden say to a man named MacCulain that The Grey of Macha had neighed in his sleep and the sword of Laeg clashed on the floor as he turned in his slumber."

The young man leaped from the grass.

"Sir," said he in a strained voice, "I do not understand your words, but they make my heart to dance and sing within me like a bird."

"If you listen to your heart," said the Philosopher, "you will learn every good thing, for the heart is the fountain of wisdom tossing its thoughts up to the brain which gives them form,"—and, so saying, he saluted the youth and went again on his way by the curving road.

Now the day had advanced, noon was long past, and the strong sunlight blazed ceaselessly on the world. His path was still on the high mountains, running on for a short distance and twisting perpetually to the right hand and to the left. One might scarcely call it a path, it grew so narrow. Sometimes, indeed, it almost ceased to be a path, for the grass had stolen forward inch by inch to cover up the tracks of man. There were no hedges but rough, tumbled ground only, which was patched by trailing bushes and stretched away in mounds and hummocks beyond the far horizon. There was a deep silence everywhere, not painful, for where the sun shines there is no sorrow: the only sound to be heard was the swish of long grasses against his feet as he trod, and the buzz of an occasional bee that came and was gone in an instant.

The Philosopher was very hungry, and he looked about on all sides to see if there was anything he might eat. "If I were a goat or a cow," said he, "I could eat this grass and be nourished. If I were a donkey I could crop the hard thistles which are growing on every hand, or if I were a bird I could feed on the caterpillars and creeping things which stir innumerably everywhere. But a man may not eat even in the midst of plenty, because he has departed from nature, and lives by crafty and twisted thought."

Speaking in this manner he chanced to lift his eyes from the ground and saw, far away, a solitary figure which melted into the folding earth and reappeared again in a different place. So peculiar and erratic were the movements of this figure that the Philosopher had great difficulty in following it, and, indeed, would have been unable to follow, but that the other chanced in his direction. When they came nearer he saw it was a young boy, who was dancing hither and thither in any and every direction. A bushy mound hid him for an instant, and the next they were standing face to face staring at each other. After a moment's silence the boy, who was about twelve years of age, and as beautiful as the morning, saluted the Philosopher.

"Have you lost your way, sir?" said he.

"All paths," the Philosopher replied, "are on the earth, and so one can never be lost—but I have lost my dinner."

The boy commenced to laugh.

"What are you laughing at, my son?" said the Philosopher.

"Because," he replied, "I am bringing you your dinner. I wondered what sent me out in this direction, for I generally go more to the east."

"Have you got my dinner?" said the Philosopher anxiously.

"I have," said the boy: "I ate my own dinner at home, and I put your dinner in my pocket. I thought," he explained, "that I might be hungry if I went far away."

"The gods directed you," said the Philosopher.

"They often do," said the boy, and he pulled a small parcel from his pocket.

The Philosopher instantly sat down, and the boy handed him the parcel. He opened this and found bread and cheese.

"It's a good dinner," said he, and commenced to eat.

"Would you not like a piece also, my son?"

"I would like a little piece," said the boy, and he sat down before the Philosopher, and they ate together happily.

When they had finished the Philosopher praised the gods, and then said, more to himself than to the boy:

"If I had a little drink of water I would want nothing else."

"There is a stream four paces from here," said his companion. "I will get some water in my cap," and he leaped away.

In a few moments he came back holding his cap tenderly, and the Philosopher took this and drank the water.

"I want nothing more in the world," said he, "except to talk with you. The sun is shining, the wind is pleasant, and the grass is soft. Sit down beside me again for a little time."

So the boy sat down, and the Philosopher lit his pipe.

"Do you live far from here?" said he.

"Not far," said the boy. "You could see my mother's house from this place if you were as tall as a tree, and even from the ground you can see a shape of smoke yonder that floats over our cottage."

The Philosopher looked but could see nothing.

"My eyes are not as good as yours are," said he, "because I am getting old."

"What does it feel like to be old?" said the boy.

"It feels stiff like," said the Philosopher.

"Is that all?" said the boy.

"I don't know," the Philosopher replied after a few moments' silence. "Can you tell me what it looks like to be young?"

"Why not?" said the boy, and then a slight look of perplexity crossed his face, and he continued, "I don't think I can."

"Young people," said the Philosopher, "do not know what age is, and old people forget what youth was. When you begin to grow old always think deeply of your youth, for an old man without memories is a wasted life, and nothing is worth remembering but our childhood. I will tell you some of the differences between being old and young, and then you can ask me questions, and so we will get at both sides of the matter. First, an old man gets tired quicker than a boy."

The boy thought for a moment, and then replied:

"That is not a great difference, for a boy does get very tired."

The Philosopher continued:

"An old man does not want to eat as often as a boy."

"That is not a great difference either," the boy replied, "for they both do eat. Tell me the big difference."

"I do not know it, my son; but I have always thought there was a big difference. Perhaps it is that an old man has memories of things which a boy cannot even guess at."

"But they both have memories," said the boy, laughing, "and so it is not a big difference."

"That is true," said the Philosopher. "Maybe there is not so much difference after all. Tell me things you do, and we will see if I can do them also."

"But I don't know what I do," he replied.

"You must know the things you do," said the Philosopher, "but you may not understand how to put them in order. The great trouble about any kind of examination is to know where to begin, but there are always two places in everything with which we can commence—they are the beginning and the end. From either of these points a view may be had which comprehends the entire period. So we will begin with the things you did this morning."

"I am satisfied with that," said the boy.

The Philosopher then continued:

"When you awakened this morning and went out of the house what was the first thing you did?"

The boy thought "I went out, then I picked up a stone and threw it into the field as far as I could."

"What then?" said the Philosopher.

"Then I ran after the stone to see could I catch up on it before it hit the ground."

"Yes," said the Philosopher.

"I ran so fast that I tumbled over myself into the grass."

"What did you do after that?"

"I lay where I fell and plucked handfuls of the grass with both hands and threw them on my back."

"Did you get up then?"

"No, I pressed my face into the grass and shouted a lot of times with my mouth against the ground, and then I sat up and did not move for a long time."

"Were you thinking?" said the Philosopher.

"No, I was not thinking or doing anything."

"Why did you do all these things?" said the Philosopher.

"For no reason at all," said the boy.

"That," said the Philosopher triumphantly, "is the difference between age and youth. Boys do things for no reason, and old people do not. I wonder do we get old because we do things by reason instead of instinct?"

"I don't know," said the boy, "everything gets old. Have you travelled very far to-day, sir?"

"I will tell you that if you will tell me your name."

"My name," said the boy, "is MacCushin."

"When I came last night," said the Philosopher, "from the place of Angus Og in the Caste of the Sleepers I was bidden say to one named MacCushin that a son would be born to Angus Og and his wife, Caitilin, and that the sleepers of Erinn had turned in their slumbers."

The boy regarded him steadfastly.

"I know," said he, "why Angus Og sent me that message. He wants me to make a poem to the people of Erinn, so that when the Sleepers arise they will meet with friends."

"The Sleepers have arisen," said the Philosopher. "They are about us on every side. They are walking now, but they have forgotten their names and the meanings of their names. You are to tell them their names and their lineage, for I am an old man, and my work is done."

"I will make a poem some day," said the boy, "and every man will shout when he hears it."

"God be with you, my son," said the Philosopher, and he embraced the boy and went forward on his journey.

About half an hour's easy travelling brought him to a point from which he could see far down below to the pine trees of Coille Doraca. The shadowy evening had crept over the world ere he reached the wood, and when he entered the little house the darkness had already descended.

The Thin Woman of Inis Magrath met him as he entered, and was about to speak harshly of his long absence, but the Philosopher kissed her with such unaccustomed tenderness, and spoke so mildly to her, that, first, astonishment enchained her tongue, and then delight set it free in a direction to which it had long been a stranger.

"Wife," said the Philosopher, "I cannot say how joyful I am to see your good face again."

The Thin Woman was unable at first to reply to this salutation, but, with incredible speed, she put on a pot of stirabout, began to bake a cake, and tried to roast potatoes. After a little while she wept loudly, and proclaimed that the world did not contain the equal of her husband for comeliness and goodness, and that she was herself a sinful person unworthy of the kindness of the gods or of such a mate.

But while the Philosopher was embracing Seumas and Brigid Beg, the door was suddenly burst open with a great noise, four policemen entered the little room, and after one dumbfoundered minute they retreated again bearing the Philosopher with them to answer a charge of murder.

BOOK 5
THE POLICEMEN

Chapter 14

S ome distance down the road the policemen halted. The night had fallen before they effected their capture, and now, in the gathering darkness, they were not at ease. In the first place, they knew that the occupation upon which they were employed was not a creditable one to a man whatever it might be to a policeman. The seizure of a criminal may be justified by certain arguments as to the health of society and the preservation of property, but no person wishes under any circumstances to hale a wise man to prison. They were further distressed by the knowledge that they were in the very centre of a populous fairy country, and that on every side the elemental hosts might be ranging, ready to fall upon them with the terrors of war or the still more awful scourge of their humour. The path leading to their station was a long one, winding through great alleys of trees, which in some places overhung the road so thickly that even the full moon could not search out that deep blackness. In the daylight these men would have arrested an Archangel and, if necessary, bludgeoned him, but in the night-time a thousand fears afflicted and a multitude of sounds shocked them from every quarter.

Two men were holding the Philosopher, one on either side; the other two walked one before and one behind him. In this order they were proceeding when just in front through the dim light they saw the road swallowed up by one of these groves already spoken of. When they came nigh they halted irresolutely: the man who was in front (a silent and perturbed sergeant) turned fiercely to the others "Come on, can't you?" said he; "what the devil are you waiting for?" and he strode forward into the black gape.

"Keep a good hold of that man," said the one behind.

"Don't be talking out of you," replied he on the right. "Haven't we got a good grip of him, and isn't he an old man into the bargain?"

"Well, keep a good tight grip of him, anyhow, for if he gave you the slip in there he'd vanish like a weasel in a bush. Them old fellows do be slippery customers. Look here, mister," said he to the Philosopher, "if you try to run away from us I'll give you a clout on the head with my baton; do you mind me now!"

They had taken only a few paces forward when the sound of hasty footsteps brought them again to a halt, and in a moment the sergeant came striding back. He was angry.

"Are you going to stay there the whole night, or what are you going to do at all?" said he.

"Let you be quiet now," said another; "we were only settling with the man here the way he wouldn't try to give us the slip in a dark place."

"Is it thinking of giving us the slip he is?" said the sergeant. "Take your baton in your hand, Shawn, and if he turns his head to one side of him hit him on that side."

"I'll do that," said Shawn, and he pulled out his truncheon.

The Philosopher had been dazed by the suddenness of these occurrences, and the enforced rapidity of his movements prevented him from either thinking or speaking, but during this brief stoppage his scattered wits began to return to their allegiance. First, bewilderment at his enforcement had seized him, and the four men, who were continually running round him and speaking all at once, and each pulling him in a different direction, gave him the impression that he was surrounded by a great rabble of people, but he could not discover what they wanted. After a time he found that there were only four men, and gathered from their remarks that he was being arrested for murder—this precipitated him into another and a deeper gulf of bewilderment. He was unable to conceive why they should arrest him for murder when he had not committed any; and, following this, he became indignant.

"I will not go another step," said he, "unless you tell me where you are bringing me and what I am accused of."

"Tell me," said the sergeant, "what did you kill them with? for it's a miracle how they came to their ends without as much as a mark on their skins or a broken tooth itself."

"Who are you talking about?" the Philosopher demanded.

"It's mighty innocent you are," he replied. "Who would I be talking about but the man and woman that used to be living with you beyond in the little house? Is it poison you gave them now, or what was it? Take a hold of your note-book, Shawn."

"Can't you have sense, man?" said Shawn. "How would I be writing in the middle of a dark place and me without as much as a pencil, let alone a book?"

"Well, we'll take it down at the station, and himself can tell us all about it as we go along. Move on now, for this is no place to be conversing in."

They paced on again, and in another moment they were swallowed up by the darkness. When they had proceeded for a little distance there came a peculiar sound in front like the breathing of some enormous animal, and also a kind of shuffling noise, and so they again halted.

"There's a queer kind of a thing in front of us," said one of the men in a low voice.

"If I had a match itself," said another.

The sergeant had also halted.

"Draw well into the side of the road," said he, "and poke your batons in front of you. Keep a tight hold of that man, Shawn."

"I'll do that," said Shawn.

Just then one of them found a few matches in his pocket, and he struck a light; there was no wind, so that it blazed easily enough, and they all peered in front. A big black cart-horse was lying in the middle of the road having a gentle sleep, and when the light shone it scrambled to its feet and went thundering away in a panic.

"Isn't that enough to put the heart crossways in you?" said one of the men, with a great sigh.

"Ay," said another; "if you stepped on that beast in the darkness you wouldn't know what to be thinking."

"I don't quite remember the way about here," said the sergeant after a while, "but I think we should take the first turn to the right. I wonder have we passed the turn yet; these criss-cross kinds of roads are the devil, and it dark as well. Do any of you men know the way?"

"I don't," said one voice; "I'm a Cavan man myself."

"Roscommon," said another, "is my country, and I wish I was there now, so I do."

"Well, if we walk straight on we're bound to get somewhere, so step it out. Have you got a good hold of that man, Shawn?"

"I have so," said Shawn.

The Philosopher's voice came pealing through the darkness.

"There is no need to pinch me, sir," said he.

"I'm not pinching you at all," said the man.

"You are so," returned the Philosopher. "You have a big lump of skin doubled up in the sleeve of my coat, and unless you instantly release it I will sit down in the road."

"Is that any better?" said the man, relaxing his hold a little.

"You have only let out half of it," replied the Philosopher. "That's better now," he continued, and they resumed their journey.

After a few minutes of silence the Philosopher began to speak.

"I do not see any necessity in nature for policemen," said he, "nor do I understand how the custom first originated. Dogs and cats do not employ these extraordinary mercenaries, and yet their polity is progressive and orderly. Crows are a gregarious race with settled habitations and an organized commonwealth. They usually congregate in a ruined tower or on the top of a church, and their civilization is based on mutual aid and tolerance for each other's idiosyncrasies. Their exceeding mobility and hardiness renders them dangerous to attack, and thus they are free to devote themselves to the development of their domestic laws and customs. If policemen were necessary to a civilization crows would certainly have evolved them, but I triumphantly insist that they have not got any policemen in their republic—"

"I don't understand a word you are saying," said the sergeant.

"It doesn't matter," said the Philosopher. "Ants and bees also live in specialized communities and have an extreme complexity both of function and occupation. Their experience in governmental matters is enormous, and yet they have never discovered that a police force is at all essential to their wellbeing—"

"Do you know," said the sergeant, "that whatever you say now will be used in evidence against you later on?"

"I do not," said the Philosopher. "It may be said that these races are free from crime, that such vices as they have are organized and communal instead of individual and anarchistic, and that, consequently, there is no necessity for policecraft, but I cannot believe that these large aggregations of people could have attained their present high culture without an interval of both national and individual dishonesty—"

"Tell me now, as you are talking," said the sergeant, "did you buy the poison at a chemist's shop, or did you smother the pair of them with a pillow?"

"I did not," said the Philosopher. "If crime is a condition precedent to the evolution of policemen, then I will submit that jackdaws are a very thievish clan—they are somewhat larger than a blackbird, and will steal wool off a sheep's back to line their nests with; they have, furthermore, been known to abstract one shilling in copper and secrete this booty so ingeniously that it has never since been recovered—"

"I had a jackdaw myself," said one of the men. "I got it from a woman that came to the door with a basket for fourpence. My mother stood on its back one day, and she getting out of bed. I split its tongue with a threepenny bit the way it would talk, but devil the word it ever said for me. It used to hop around letting on it had a lame leg, and then it would steal your socks."

"Shut up!" roared the sergeant.

"If," said the Philosopher, "these people steal both from from sheep and from men, if their peculations range from wool to money, I do not see how they can avoid stealing from each other, and consequently, if anywhere, it is amongst jackdaws one should look for the growth of a police force, but there is no such force in existence. The real reason is that they are a witty and thoughtful race who look temperately on what is known as crime and evil—one eats, one steals; it is all in the order of things, and therefore not to be quarrelled with. There is no other view possible to a philosophical people—"

"What the devil is he talking about?" said the sergeant.

"Monkeys are gregarious and thievish and semi-human. They inhabit the equatorial latitudes and eat nuts—"

"Do you know what he is saying, Shawn?"

"I do not," said Shawn.

"—they ought to have evolved professional thief-takers, but it is common knowledge that they have not done so. Fishes, squirrels, rats, beavers, and bison have also abstained from this singular growth—therefore, when I insist that I see no necessity for policemen and object to their presence, I base that objection on logic and facts, and not on any immediate petty prejudice."

"Shawn," said the sergeant, "have you got a good grip on that man?"

"I have," said Shawn.

"Well, if he talks any more hit him with your baton."

"I will so," said Shawn.

"There's a speck of light down yonder, and, maybe, it's a candle in a window—we'll ask the way at that place."

In about three minutes they came to a small house which was overhung by trees. If the light had not been visible they would undoubtedly have passed it in the darkness. As they approached the door the sound of a female voice came to them scoldingly.

"There's somebody up anyhow," said the sergeant, and he tapped at the door.

The scolding voice ceased instantly. After a few seconds he tapped again; then a voice was heard from just behind the door.

"Tomas," said the voice, "go and bring up the two dogs with you before I take the door off the chain."

The door was then opened a few inches and a face peered out "What would you be wanting at this hour of the night?" said the woman.

"Not much, ma'am," said the sergeant; "only a little direction about the road, for we are not sure whether we've gone too far or not far enough."

The woman noticed their uniforms.

"Is it policemen ye are? There's no harm in your coming in, I suppose, and if a drink of milk is any good to ye I have plenty of it."

"Milk's better than nothing," said the sergeant with a sigh.

"I've a little sup of spirits," said she, "but it wouldn't be enough to go around."

"Ah, well," said he, looking sternly at his comrades, "everybody has to take their chance in this world," and he stepped into the house followed by his men.

The women gave him a little sup of whisky from a bottle, and to each of the other men she gave a cup of milk.

"It'll wash the dust out of our gullets, anyhow," said one of them.

There were two chairs, a bed, and a table in the room. The Philosopher and his attendants sat on the bed. The sergeant sat on the table, the fourth man took a chair, and the woman dropped wearily into the remaining chair from which she looked with pity at the prisoner.

"What are you taking the poor man away for?" she asked.

"He's a bad one, ma'am," said the sergeant. "He killed a man and a woman that were staying with him and he buried their corpses underneath the hearthstone of his house. He's a real malefactor, mind you."

"Is it hanging him you'll be, God help us?"

"You never know, and I wouldn't be a bit surprised if it came to that. But you were in trouble yourself, ma'am, for we heard your voice lamenting about something as we came along the road."

"I was, indeed," she replied, "for the person that has a son in her house has a trouble in her heart."

"Do you tell me now—What did he do on you?" and the sergeant bent a look of grave reprobation on a young lad who was standing against the wall between two dogs.

"He's a good boy enough in some ways," said she, "but he's too fond of beasts. He'll go and lie in the kennel along with them two dogs for hours at a time, petting them and making a lot of them, but if I try to give him a kiss, or to hug him for a couple of minutes when I do be tired after the work, he'll wriggle like an eel till I let him out—it would make a body hate him, so it would. Sure, there's no nature in him, sir, and I'm his mother."

"You ought to be ashamed of yourself, you young whelp," said the sergeant very severely.

"And then there's the horse," she continued. "Maybe you met it down the road a while ago?"

"We did, ma'am," said the sergeant.

"Well, when he came in Tomas went to tie him up, for he's a caution at getting out and wandering about the road, the way you'd break your neck over him if you weren't minding. After a while I told the boy to come in, but he didn't come, so I went out myself, and there was himself and the horse with their arms round each other's necks looking as if they were moonstruck."

"Faith, he's the queer lad!" said the sergeant. "What do you be making love to the horse for, Tomas?"

"It was all I could do to make him come in," she continued, "and then I said to him, 'Sit down alongside of me here, Tomas, and keep me company for a little while'—for I do be lonely in the night-time—but he wouldn't stay quiet at all. One minute he'd say, 'Mother, there's a moth flying round the candle and it'll be burnt,' and then, 'There was a fly going into the spider's web in the corner,' and he'd have to save it, and after that, 'There's a daddy-long-legs hurting himself on the window-pane,' and he'd have to let it out; but when I try to kiss him he pushes me away. My heart is tormented, so it is, for what have I in the world but him?"

"Is his father dead, ma'am?" said the sergeant kindly.

"I'll tell the truth," said she. "I don't know whether he is or not, for a long time ago, when we used to live in the city of Bla' Cliah, he lost his work one time and he never came back to me again. He was ashamed to come home I'm thinking, the poor man, because he had no money; as if I would have minded whether he had any money or not—sure, he was very fond of me, sir, and we could have pulled along somehow. After that I came back to my father's place here; the rest of the children died on me, and then my father died, and I'm doing the best I can by myself. It's only that I'm a little bit troubled with the boy now and again."

"It's a hard case, ma'am," said the sergeant, "but maybe the boy is only a bit wild not having his father over him, and maybe it's just that he's used to yourself, for there isn't a child at all that doesn't love his mother. Let you behave yourself now, Tomas; attend to your mother, and leave the beasts and the insects alone, like a decent boy, for there's no insect in the world will ever like you as well as she does. Could you tell me, ma'am, if we have passed the first turn on this road, or is it in front of us still, for we are lost altogether in the darkness?"

"It's in front of you still," she replied, "about ten minutes down the road; you can't miss it, for you'll see the sky where there is a gap in the trees, and that gap is the turn you want."

"Thank you, ma'am," said the sergeant; "we'd better be moving on, for there's a long tramp in front of us before we get to sleep this night."

He stood up and the men rose to follow him when, suddenly, the boy spoke in a whisper.

"Mother," said he, "they are going to hang the man," and he burst into tears.

"Oh, hush, hush," said the woman, "sure, the men can't help it." She dropped quickly on her knees and opened her arms, "Come over to your mother, my darling."

The boy ran to her.

"They are going to hang him," he cried in a high, thin voice, and he plucked at her arm violently.

"Now, then, my young boy-o," said the sergeant, "none of that violence."

The boy turned suddenly and flew at him with astonishing ferocity. He hurled himself against the sergeant's legs and bit, and kicked, and struck at him. So furiously sudden was his attack that the man went staggering back against the wall, then he plucked at the boy and whirled him across the room. In an instant the two dogs leaped at him snarling with rage—one of these he kicked into a corner, from which it rebounded again bristling and red-eyed; the other dog was caught by the woman, and after a few frantic seconds she gripped the first dog also. To a horrible chorus of howls and snapping teeth the men hustled outside and slammed the door.

"Shawn," the sergeant bawled, "have you got a good grip of that man?"

"I have so," said Shawn.

"If he gets away I'll kick the belly out of you; mind that now! Come along with you and no more of your slouching."

They marched down the road in a tingling silence.

"Dogs," said the Philosopher, "are a most intelligent race of people—"

"People, my granny!" said the sergeant.

"From the earliest ages their intelligence has been observed and recorded, so that ancient literatures are bulky with references to their sagacity and fidelity—"

"Will you shut your old jaw?" said the sergeant.

"I will not," said the Philosopher. "Elephants also are credited with an extreme intelligence and devotion to their masters, and they will build a wall or nurse a baby with equal skill and happiness. Horses have received high recommendations in this respect, but crocodiles, hens, beetles, armadillos, and fish do not evince any remarkable partiality for man—"

"I wish," said the sergeant bitterly, "that all them beasts were stuffed down your throttle the way you'd have to hold your prate."

"It doesn't matter," said the Philosopher. "I do not know why these animals should attach themselves to men with gentleness and love and yet be able to preserve intact their initial bloodthirstiness, so that while they will allow their masters to misuse them in any way they will yet fight most willingly with each other, and are never really happy saving in the conduct of some private and nonsensical battle of their own. I do not believe that it is fear which tames these creatures into mildness, but that the most savage animal has a capacity for love which has not been sufficiently noted, and which, if more intelligent attention had been directed upon it, would have raised them to the status of intellectual animals as against intelligent ones, and, perhaps, have opened to us a correspondence which could not have been other than beneficial."

"Keep your eyes out for that gap in the trees, Shawn," said the sergeant.

"I'm doing that," said Shawn.

The Philosopher continued:

"Why can I not exchange ideas with a cow? I am amazed at the incompleteness of my growth when I and a fellow-creature stand dumbly before each other without one glimmer of comprehension, locked and barred from all friendship and intercourse—"

"Shawn," cried the sergeant.

"Don't interrupt," said the Philosopher; "you are always talking.— The lower animals, as they are foolishly called, have abilities at which we can only wonder. The mind of an ant is one to which I would readily go to school. Birds have atmospheric and levitational information which millions of years will not render accessible to us; who that has seen a spider weaving his labyrinth, or a bee voyaging safely in the trackless air, can refuse to credit that a vivid, trained intelligence animates these small enigmas? and the commonest earthworm is the heir to a culture before which I bow with the profoundest veneration—"

"Shawn," said the sergeant, "say something for goodness' sake to take the sound of that man's clack out of my ear."

"I wouldn't know what to be talking about," said Shawn, "for I never was much of a hand at conversation, and, barring my prayers, I got no education—I think myself that he was making a remark about a dog. Did you ever own a dog, sergeant?"

"You are doing very well, Shawn," said the sergeant, "keep it up now."

"I knew a man had a dog would count up to a hundred for you. He won lots of money in bets about it, and he'd have made a fortune, only that I noticed one day he used to be winking at the dog, and when he'd stop winking the dog would stop counting. We made him turn his back after that, and got the dog to count sixpence, but he barked for more than five shillings, he did so, and he would have counted up to a pound, maybe, only that his master turned round and hit him a kick. Every person that ever paid him a bet said they wanted their money back, but the man went away to America in the night, and I expect he's doing well there for he took the dog with him. It was a wire-haired terrier bitch, and it was the devil for having pups."

"It is astonishing," said the Philosopher, "on what slender compulsion people will go to America—"

"Keep it up, Shawn," said the sergeant, "you are doing me a favour."

"I will so," said Shawn. "I had a cat one time and it used to have kittens every two months."

The Philosopher's voice arose:

"If there was any periodicity about these migrations one could understand them. Birds, for example, migrate from their homes in the late autumn and seek abroad the sustenance and warmth which the winter would withhold if they remained in their native lands. The salmon also, a dignified fish with a pink skin, emigrates from the Atlantic Ocean, and betakes himself inland to the streams and lakes, where he recuperates for a season, and is often surprised by net, angle, or spear—"

"Cut in now, Shawn," said the sergeant anxiously.

Shawn began to gabble with amazing speed and in a mighty voice:

"Cats sometimes eat their kittens, and sometimes they don't. A cat that eats its kittens is a heartless brute. I knew a cat used to eat its kittens—it had four legs and a long tail, and it used to get the head-staggers every time it had eaten its kittens. I killed it myself one day with a hammer for I couldn't stand the smell it made, so I couldn't—"

"Shawn," said the sergeant, "can't you talk about something else besides cats and dogs?"

"Sure, I don't know what to talk about," said Shawn. "I'm sweating this minute trying to please you, so I arm. If you'll tell me what to talk about I'll do my endeavours."

"You're a fool," said the sergeant sorrowfully; "you'll never make a constable. I'm thinking that I would sooner listen to the man himself than to you. Have you got a good hold of him now?"

"I have so," said Shawn.

"Well, step out and maybe we'll reach the barracks this night, unless this is a road that there isn't any end to at all. What was that? Did you hear a noise?"

"I didn't hear a thing," said Shawn.

"I thought," said another man, "that I heard something moving in the hedge at the side of the road."

"That's what I heard," said the sergeant. "Maybe it was a weasel. I wish to the devil that we were out of this place where you can't see as much as your own nose. Now did you hear it, Shawn?"

"I did so," said Shawn; "there's some one in the hedge, for a weasel would make a different kind of a noise if it made any at all."

"Keep together, men," said the sergeant, "and march on; if there's anybody about they've no business with us."

He had scarcely spoken when there came a sudden pattering of feet, and immediately the four men were surrounded and were being struck at on every side with sticks and hands and feet.

"Draw your batons," the sergeant roared; "keep a good grip of that man, Shawn."

"I will so," said Shawn.

"Stand round him, you other men, and hit anything that comes near you."

There was no sound of voices from the assailants, only a rapid scuffle of feet, the whistle of sticks as they swung through the air or slapped smartly against a body or clashed upon each other, and the quick breathing of many people; but from the four policemen there came noise and to spare as they struck wildly on every side, cursing the darkness and their opposers with fierce enthusiasm.

"Let out," cried Shawn suddenly. "Let out or I'll smash your nut for you. There's some one pulling at the prisoner, and I've dropped my baton."

The truncheons of the policemen had been so ferociously exercised that their antagonists departed as swiftly and as mysteriously as they came. It was just two minutes of frantic, aimless conflict, and then the silent night was round them again, without any sound but the slow creaking of branches, the swish of leaves as they swung and poised, and the quiet croon of the wind along the road.

"Come on, men," said the sergeant, "we'd better be getting out of this place as quick as we can. Are any of ye hurted?"

"I've got one of the enemy," said Shawn, panting.

"You've got what?" said the sergeant.

"I've got one of them, and he is wriggling like an eel on a pan."

"Hold him tight," said the sergeant excitedly.

"I will so," said Shawn. "It's a little one by the feel of it. If one of ye would hold the prisoner, I'd get a better grip on this one. Aren't they dangerous villains now?"

Another man took hold of the Philosopher's arm, and Shawn got both hands on his captive.

"Keep quiet, I'm telling you," said he, "or I'll throttle you, I will so. Faith, it seems like a little boy by the feel of it!"

"A little boy!" said the sergeant.

"Yes, he doesn't reach up to my waist."

"It must be the young brat from the cottage that set the dogs on us, the one that loves beasts. Now then, boy, what do you mean by this kind of thing? You'll find yourself in gaol for this, my young buck-o. Who was with you, eh? Tell me that now?" and the sergeant bent forward.

"Hold up your head, sonny, and talk to the sergeant," said Shawn. "Oh!" he roared, and suddenly he made a little rush forward. "I've got him," he gasped; "he nearly got away. It isn't a boy at all, sergeant; there's whiskers on it!"

"What do you say?" said the sergeant.

"I put my hand under its chin and there's whiskers on it. I nearly let him out with the surprise, I did so."

"Try again," said the sergeant in a low voice; "you are making a mistake."

"I don't like touching them," said Shawn. "It's a soft whisker like a billy-goat's. Maybe you'd try yourself, sergeant, for I tell you I'm frightened of it."

"Hold him over here," said the sergeant, "and keep a good grip of him."

"I'll do that," said Shawn, and he hauled some reluctant object towards his superior.

The sergeant put out his hand and touched a head.

"It's only a boy's size to be sure," said he, then he slid his hand down the face and withdrew it quickly.

"There are whiskers on it," said he soberly. "What the devil can it be? I never met whiskers so near the ground before. Maybe they are false ones, and it's just the boy yonder trying to disguise himself." He put out his hand again with an effort, felt his way to the chin, and tugged.

Instantly there came a yell, so loud, so sudden, that every man of them jumped in a panic.

"They are real whiskers," said the sergeant with a sigh. "I wish I knew what it is. His voice is big enough for two men, and that's a fact. Have you got another match on you?"

"I have two more in my waistcoat pocket," said one of the men.

"Give me one of them," said the sergeant; "I'll strike it myself."

He groped about until he found the hand with the match.

"Be sure and hold him tight, Shawn, the way we can have a good look at him, for this is like to be a queer miracle of a thing."

"I'm holding him by the two arms," said Shawn, "he can't stir anything but his head, and I've got my chest on that."

The sergeant struck the match, shading it for a moment with his hand, then he turned it on their new prisoner.

They saw a little man dressed in tight green clothes; he had a broad pale face with staring eyes, and there was a thin fringe of grey whisker under his chin—then the match went out.

"It's a Leprecaun," said the sergeant.

The men were silent for a full couple of minutes—at last Shawn spoke.

"Do you tell me so?" said he in a musing voice; "that's a queer miracle altogether."

"I do," said the sergeant. "Doesn't it stand to reason that it can't be anything else? You saw it yourself."

Shawn plumped down on his knees before his captive.

"Tell me where the money is?" he hissed. "Tell me where the money is or I'll twist your neck off."

The other men also gathered eagerly around, shouting threats and commands at the Leprecaun.

"Hold your whist," said Shawn fiercely to them. "He can't answer the lot of you, can he?" and he turned again to the Leprecaun and shook him until his teeth chattered.

"If you don't tell me where the money is at once I'll kill you, I will so."

"I haven't got any money at all, sir," said the Leprecaun.

"None of your lies," roared Shawn. "Tell the truth now or it'll be worse for you."

"I haven't got any money," said the Leprecaun, "for Meehawl MacMurrachu of the Hill stole our crock a while back, and he buried it under a thorn bush. I can bring you to the place if you don't believe me."

"Very good," said Shawn. "Come on with me now, and I'll clout you if you as much as wriggle; do you mind me?"

"What would I wriggle for?" said the Leprecaun: "sure I like being with you."

Hereupon the sergeant roared at the top of his voice.

"Attention," said he, and the men leaped to position like automata.

"What is it you are going to do with your prisoner, Shawn?" said he sarcastically. "Don't you think we've had enough tramping of these roads for one night, now? Bring up that Leprecaun to the barracks or it'll be the worse for you—do you hear me talking to you?"

"But the gold, sergeant," said Shawn sulkily.

"If there's any gold it'll be treasure trove, and belong to the Crown. What kind of a constable are you at all, Shawn? Mind what you are about now, my man, and no back answers. Step along there. Bring that murderer up at once, whichever of you has him."

There came a gasp from the darkness.

"Oh, Oh, Oh!" said a voice of horror.

"What's wrong with you?" said the sergeant: "are you hurted?"

"The prisoner!" he gasped, "he, he's got away!"

"Got away?" and the sergeant's voice was a blare of fury.

"While we were looking at the Leprecaun," said the voice of woe, "I must have forgotten about the other one—I, I haven't got him—"

"You gawm!" gritted the sergeant.

"Is it my prisoner that's gone?" said Shawn in a deep voice. He leaped forward with a curse and smote his negligent comrade so terrible a blow in the face, that the man went flying backwards, and the thud of his head on the road could have been heard anywhere.

"Get up," said Shawn, "get up till I give you another one."

"That will do," said the sergeant, "we'll go home. We're the laughing-stock of the world. I'll pay you out for this some time, every damn man of ye. Bring that Leprecaun along with you, and quick march."

"Oh!" said Shawn in a strangled tone.

"What is it now?" said the sergeant testily.

"Nothing," replied Shawn.

"What did you say 'Oh!' for then, you block-head?"

"It's the Leprecaun, sergeant," said Shawn in a whisper—"he's got away—when I was hitting the man there I forgot all about the Leprecaun: he must have run into the hedge. Oh, sergeant, dear, don't say anything to me now—!"

"Quick march," said the sergeant, and the four men moved on through the darkness in a silence, which was only skin deep.

Chapter 15

By reason of the many years which he had spent in the gloomy pine wood, the Philosopher could see a little in the darkness, and when he found there was no longer any hold on his coat he continued his journey quietly, marching along with his head sunken on his breast in a deep abstraction. He was meditating on the word "Me," and endeavouring to pursue it through all its changes and adventures. The fact of "me-ness" was one which startled him. He was amazed at his own being. He knew that the hand which he held up and pinched with another hand was not him and the endeavour to find out what was him was one which had frequently exercised his leisure. He had not gone far when there came a tug at his sleeve and looking down he found one of the Leprecauns of the Gort trotting by his side.

"Noble Sir," said the Leprecaun, "you are terrible hard to get into conversation with. I have been talking to you for the last long time and you won't listen."

"I am listening now," replied the Philosopher.

"You are, indeed," said the Leprecaun heartily. "My brothers are on the other side of the road over there beyond the hedge, and they want to talk to you: will you come with me, Noble Sir?"

"Why wouldn't I go with you?" said the Philosopher, and he turned aside with the Leprecaun.

They pushed softly through a gap in the hedge and into a field beyond.

"Come this way, sir," said his guide, and the Philosopher followed him across the field. In a few minutes they came to a thick bush among the leaves of which the other Leprecauns were hiding. They thronged out to meet the Philosopher's approach and welcomed him with every appearance of joy. With them was the Thin Woman of Inis Magrath, who embraced her husband tenderly and gave thanks for his escape.

"The night is young yet," remarked one of the Leprecauns. "Let us sit down here and talk about what should be done."

"I am tired enough," said the Philosopher, "for I have been travelling all yesterday, and all this day and the whole of this night I have been going also, so I would be glad to sit down anywhere."

They sat down under the bush and the Philosopher lit his pipe. In the open space where they were there was just light enough to see the smoke coming from his pipe, but scarcely more. One recognized a figure as a deeper shadow than the surrounding darkness; but as the ground was dry and the air just touched with a pleasant chill, there was no discomfort. After the Philosopher had drawn a few mouthfuls of smoke he passed his pipe on to the next person, and in this way his pipe made the circuit of the party.

"When I put the children to bed," said the Thin Woman, "I came down the road in your wake with a basin of stirabout, for you had no time to take your food, God help you! and I was thinking you must have been hungry."

"That is so," said the Philosopher in a very anxious voice: "but I don't blame you, my dear, for letting the basin fall on the road—"

"While I was going along," she continued, "I met these good people and when I told them what happened they came with me to see if anything could be done. The time they ran out of the hedge to fight the policemen I wanted to go with them, but I was afraid the stirabout would be spilt."

The Philosopher licked his lips.

"I am listening to you, my love," said he.

"So I had to stay where I was with the stirabout under my shawl—"

"Did you slip then, dear wife?"

"I did not, indeed," she replied: "I have the stirabout with me this minute. It's rather cold, I'm thinking, but it is better than nothing at all," and she placed the bowl in his hands.

"I put sugar in it," said she shyly, "and currants, and I have a spoon in my pocket."

"It tastes well," said the Philosopher, and he cleaned the basin so speedily that his wife wept because of his hunger.

By this time the pipe had come round to him again and it was welcomed.

"Now we can talk," said he, and he blew a great cloud of smoke into the darkness and sighed happily.

"We were thinking," said the Thin Woman, "that you won't be able to come back to our house for a while yet: the policemen will be peeping about Coille Doraca for a long time, to be sure; for isn't it true that if there is a good thing coming to a person, nobody takes much trouble to find him, but if there is a bad thing or a punishment in store for a man, then the whole world will be searched until he be found?"

"It is a true statement," said the Philosopher.

"So what we arranged was this—that you should go to live with these little men in their house under the yew tree of the Gort. There is not a policeman in the world would find you there; or if you went by night to the Brugh of the Boyne, Angus Og himself would give you a refuge."

One of the Leprecauns here interposed.

"Noble Sir," said he, "there isn't much room in our house but there's no stint of welcome in it. You would have a good time with us travelling on moonlit nights and seeing strange things, for we often go to visit the Shee of the Hills and they come to see us; there is always something to talk about, and we have dances in the caves and on the tops of the hills. Don't be imagining now that we have a poor life for there is fun and plenty with us and the Brugh of Angus Mac an Og is hard to be got at."

"I would like to dance, indeed," returned the Philosopher, "for I do believe that dancing is the first and last duty of man. If we cannot be gay what can we be? Life is not any use at all unless we find a laugh here and there—but this time, decent men of the Gort, I cannot go with you, for it is laid on me to give myself up to the police."

"You would not do that," exclaimed the Thin Woman pitifully: "You wouldn't think of doing that now!"

"An innocent man," said he, "cannot be oppressed, for he is fortified by his mind and his heart cheers him. It is only on a guilty person that the rigour of punishment can fall, for he punishes himself. This is what I think, that a man should always obey the law with his body and always disobey it with his mind. I have been arrested, the men of the law had me in their hands, and I will have to go back to them so that they may do whatever they have to do."

The Philosopher resumed his pipe, and although the others reasoned with him for a long time they could not by any means remove him from his purpose. So, when the pale glimmer of dawn had stolen over the sky, they arose and went downwards to the cross-roads and so to the Police Station.

Outside the village the Leprecauns bade him farewell and the Thin Woman also took her leave of him, saying she would visit Angus Og and implore his assistance on behalf of her husband, and then the Leprecauns and the Thin Woman returned again the way they came, and the Philosopher walked on to the barracks.

Chapter 16

When he knocked at the barracks door it was opened by a man with tousled, red hair, who looked as though he had just awakened from sleep.

"What do you want at this hour of the night?" said he.

"I want to give myself up," said the Philosopher. The policeman looked at him "A man as old as you are," said he, "oughtn't to be a fool. Go home now, I advise you, and don't say a word to any one whether you did it or not. Tell me this now, was it found out, or are you only making a clean breast of it?"

"Sure I must give myself up," said the Philosopher.

"If you must, you must, and that's an end of it. Wipe your feet on the rail there and come in—I'll take your deposition."

"I have no deposition for you," said the Philosopher, "for I didn't do a thing at all."

The policeman stared at him again.

"If that's so," said he, "you needn't come in at all, and you needn't have wakened me out of my sleep either. Maybe, tho', you are the man that fought the badger on the Naas Road—Eh?"

"I am not," replied the Philosopher: "but I was arrested for killing my brother and his wife, although I never touched them."

"Is that who you are?" said the policeman; and then, briskly, "You're as welcome as the cuckoo, you are so. Come in and make yourself comfortable till the men awaken, and they are the lads that'll be glad to see you. I couldn't make head or tail of what they said when they came in last night, and no one else either, for they did nothing but fight each other and curse the banshees and cluricauns of Leinster. Sit down there on the settle by the fire and, maybe, you'll be able to get a sleep; you look as if you were tired, and the mud of every county in Ireland is on your boots."

The Philosopher thanked him and stretched out on the settle. In a short time, for he was very weary, he fell asleep.

Many hours later he was awakened by the sound of voices, and found on rising, that the men who had captured him on the previous evening were standing by the bed. The sergeant's face beamed with joy. He was dressed only in his trousers and shirt. His hair was sticking up in some places and sticking out in others which gave a certain wild look to him, and his feet were bare. He took the Philosopher's two hands in his own and swore if ever there was anything he could do to comfort him he would do that and more. Shawn, in a similar state of unclothedness, greeted the Philosopher and proclaimed himself his friend and follower for ever. Shawn further announced that he did not believe the Philosopher had killed the two people, that if he had killed them they must have richly deserved it, and that if he was hung he would plant flowers on his grave; for a decenter, quieter, and wiser man he had never met and never would meet in the world.

These professions of esteem comforted the Philosopher, and he replied to them in terms which made the red-haired policeman gape in astonishment and approval.

He was given a breakfast of bread and cocoa which he ate with his guardians, and then, as they had to take up their outdoor duties, he was conducted to the backyard and informed he could walk about there and that he might smoke until he was black in the face. The policemen severally presented him with a pipe, a tin of tobacco, two boxes of matches and a dictionary, and then they withdrew, leaving him to his own devices.

The garden was about twelve feet square, having high, smooth walls on every side, and into it there came neither sun nor wind. In one corner a clump of rusty-looking sweet-pea was climbing up the wall— every leaf of this plant was riddled with holes, and there were no flowers on it. Another corner was occupied by dwarf nasturtiums, and on this plant, in despite of every discouragement, two flowers were blooming, but its leaves also were tattered and dejected. A mass of ivy clung to the third corner, its leaves were big and glossy at the top, but near the ground there was only grey, naked stalks laced together by cobwebs. The fourth wall was clothed in a loose Virginia creeper every leaf of which looked like an insect that could crawl if it wanted to. The centre of this small plot had used every possible artifice to cover itself with grass, and in some places it had wonderfully succeeded, but the pieces of broken bottles, shattered jampots, and sections of crockery were so numerous that no attempt at growth could be other than tentative and unpassioned.

Here, for a long time, the Philosopher marched up and down. At one moment he examined the sweet-pea and mourned with it on a wretched existence. Again he congratulated the nasturtium on its two bright children; but he thought of the gardens wherein they might have bloomed and the remembrance of that spacious, sunny freedom saddened him.

"Indeed, poor creatures!" said he, "ye also are in gaol."

The blank, soundless yard troubled him so much that at last he called to the red-haired policeman and begged to be put into a cell in preference; and to the common cell he was, accordingly, conducted.

This place was a small cellar built beneath the level of the ground. An iron grating at the top of the wall admitted one blanched wink of light, but the place was bathed in obscurity. A wooden ladder led down to the cell from a hole in the ceiling, and this hole also gave a spark of brightness and some little air to the room. The walls were of stone covered with plaster, but the plaster had fallen away in many places leaving the rough stones visible at every turn of the eye.

There were two men in the cell, and these the Philosopher saluted; but they did not reply, nor did they speak to each other. There was a low, wooden form fixed to the wall, running quite round the room, and on this, far apart from each other, the two men were seated, with their elbows resting on their knees, their heads propped upon their hands, and each of them with an unwavering gaze fixed on the floor between his feet.

The Philosopher walked for a time up and down the little cell, but soon he also sat down on the low form, propped his head on his hands and lapsed to a melancholy dream.

So the day passed. Twice a policeman came down the ladder bearing three portions of food, bread and cocoa; and by imperceptible gradations the light faded away from the grating and the darkness came. After a great interval the policeman again approached carrying three mattresses and three rough blankets, and these he bundled through the hole. Each of the men took a mattress and a blanket and spread them on the floor, and the Philosopher took his share also.

By this time they could not see each other and all their operations were conducted by the sense of touch alone. They laid themselves down on the beds and a terrible, dark silence brooded over the room.

But the Philosopher could not sleep, he kept his eyes shut, for the darkness under his eyelids was not so dense as that which surrounded him; indeed, he could at will illuminate his own darkness and order around him the sunny roads or the sparkling sky. While his eyes were closed he had the mastery of all pictures of light and colour and warmth, but an irresistible fascination compelled him every few minutes to reopen them, and in the sad space around he could not create any happiness. The darkness weighed very sadly upon him so that in a short time it did creep under his eyelids and drowned his happy pictures until a blackness possessed him both within and without "Can one's mind go to prison as well as one's body?" said he.

He strove desperately to regain his intellectual freedom, but he could not. He could conjure up no visions but those of fear. The creatures of the dark invaded him, fantastic terrors were thronging on every side: they came from the darkness into his eyes and beyond into himself, so that his mind as well as his fancy was captured, and he knew he was, indeed, in gaol.

It was with a great start that he heard a voice speaking from the silence—a harsh, yet cultivated voice, but he could not imagine which of his companions was speaking. He had a vision of that man tormented by the mental imprisonment of the darkness, trying to get away from his ghosts and slimy enemies, goaded into speech in his own despite lest he should be submerged and finally possessed by the abysmal demons. For a while the voice spoke of the strangeness of life and the cruelty of men to each other—disconnected sentences, odd words of selfpity and self-encouragement, and then the matter became more connected and a story grew in the dark cell "I knew a man," said the voice, "and he was a clerk. He had thirty shillings a week, and for five years he had never missed a day going to his work. He was a careful man, but a person with a wife and four children cannot save much out of thirty shillings a week. The rent of a house is high, a wife and children must be fed, and they have to get boots and clothes, so that at the end of each week that man's thirty shillings used to be all gone. But they managed to get along somehow—the man and his wife and the four children were fed and clothed and educated, and the man often wondered how so much could be done with so little money; but the reason was that his wife was a careful woman. . . and then the man got sick. A poor person cannot afford to get sick, and a married man cannot leave his work. If he is sick he has to be sick; but he must go to his work all the same, for if he stayed away who would pay the wages and feed his family? and when he went back to work he might find that there was nothing for him to do. This man fell sick, but he made no change in his way of life: he got up at the same time and went to the office as usual, and he got through the day somehow without attracting his employer's attention. He didn't know what was wrong with him: he only knew that he was sick. Sometimes he had sharp, swift pains in his head, and again there would be long hours of languor when he could scarcely bear to change his position or lift a pen. He would commence a letter with the words 'Dear Sir,' forming the letter 'D' with painful, accurate slowness, elaborating and thickening the up and down strokes, and being troubled when he had to leave that letter for the next one; he built the next letter by hair strokes and would start on the third with hatred. The end of a word seemed to that man like the conclusion of an event—it was a surprising, isolated, individual thing, having no reference to anything else in the world, and on starting a new word he seemed bound, in order to preserve its individuality, to write it in a different handwriting. He would sit with his shoulders hunched up and his pen resting on the paper, staring at a letter until he was nearly mesmerized, and then come to himself with a sense of fear, which started him working like a madman, so that he might not be behind with his business. The day seemed to be so long. It rolled on rusty hinges that could scarcely move. Each hour was like a great circle swollen with heavy air, and it droned and buzzed into an eternity. It seemed to the man that his hand in particular wanted to rest. It was luxury not to work with it. It was good to lay it down on a sheet of paper with the pen sloping against his finger, and then watch his hand going to sleep—it seemed to the man that it was his hand and not himself wanted to sleep, but it always awakened when the pen slipped. There was an instinct in him somewhere not to let the pen slip, and every time the pen moved his hand awakened, and began to work languidly. When he went home at night he lay down at once and stared for hours at a fly on the wall or a crack on the ceiling. When his wife spoke to him he heard her speaking as from a great distance, and he answered her dully as though he was replying through a cloud. He only wanted to be let alone, to be allowed to stare at the fly on the wall, or the crack on the ceiling.

"One morning he found that he couldn't get up, or rather, that he didn't want to get up. When his wife called him he made no reply, and she seemed to call him every ten seconds—the words, 'get up, get up,' were crackling all round him; they were bursting like bombs on the right hand and on the left of him: they were scattering from above and all around him, bursting upwards from the floor, swirling, swaying, and jostling each other. Then the sounds ceased, and one voice only said to him 'You are late!' He saw these words like a blur hanging in the air, just beyond his eyelids, and he stared at the blur until he fell asleep."

The voice in the cell ceased speaking for a few minutes, and then it went on again.

"For three weeks the man did not leave his bed—he lived faintly in a kind of trance, wherein great forms moved about slowly and immense words were drumming gently for ever. When he began to take notice again everything in the house was different. Most of the furniture, paid for so hardly, was gone. He missed a thing everywhere—chairs, a mirror, a table: wherever he looked he missed something; and downstairs was worse—there, everything was gone. His wife had sold all her furniture to pay for doctors, for medicine, for food and rent. And she was changed too: good things had gone from her face; she was gaunt, sharp-featured, miserable—but she was comforted to think he was going back to work soon.

"There was a flurry in his head when he went to his office. He didn't know what his employer would say for stopping away. He might blame him for being sick—he wondered would his employer pay him for the weeks he was absent. When he stood at the door he was frightened. Suddenly the thought of his master's eye grew terrible to him: it was a steady, cold, glassy eye; but he opened the door and went in. His master was there with another man and he tried to say 'Good morning, sir,' in a natural and calm voice; but he knew that the strange man had been engaged instead of himself, and this knowledge posted itself between his tongue and his thought. He heard himself stammering, he felt that his whole bearing had become drooping and abject. His master was talking swiftly and the other man was looking at him in an embarrassed, stealthy, and pleading manner: his eyes seemed to be apologising for having supplanted him—so he mumbled 'Good day, sir,' and stumbled out.

"When he got outside he could not think where to go. After a while he went in the direction of the little park in the centre of the city. It was quite near and he sat down on an iron bench facing a pond. There were children walking up and down by the water giving pieces of bread to the swans. Now and again a labouring man or a messenger went by quickly; now and again a middleaged, slovenly-dressed man drooped past aimlessly: sometimes a tattered, self-intent woman with a badgered face flopped by him. When he looked at these dull people the thought came to him that they were not walking there at all; they were trailing through hell, and their desperate eyes saw none but devils around them. He saw himself joining these battered strollers. . . and he could not think what he would tell his wife when he went home. He rehearsed to himself the terms of his dismissal a hundred times. How his master looked, what he had said: and then the fine, ironical things he had said to his master. He sat in the park all day, and when evening fell he went home at his accustomed hour.

"His wife asked him questions as to how he had got on, and wanted to know was there any chance of being paid for the weeks of absence; the man answered her volubly, ate his supper and went to bed: but he did not tell his wife that he had been dismissed and that there would be no money at the end of the week. He tried to tell her, but when he met her eye he found that he could not say the words—he was afraid of the look that might come into her face when she heard it—she, standing terrified in those dismantled rooms. . . !

"In the morning he ate his breakfast and went out again—to work, his wife thought. She bid him ask the master about the three weeks' wages, or to try and get an advance on the present week's wages, for they were hardly put to it to buy food. He said he would do his best, but he went straight to the park and sat looking at the pond, looking at the passers-by and dreaming. In the middle of the day he started up in a panic and went about the city asking for work in offices, shops, warehouses, everywhere, but he could not get any. He trailed back heavy-footed again to the park and sat down.

"He told his wife more lies about his work that night and what his master had said when he asked for an advance. He couldn't bear the children to touch him. After a little time he sneaked away to his bed.

"A week went that way. He didn't look for work any more. He sat in the park, dreaming, with his head bowed into his hands. The next day would be the day he should have been paid his wages. The next day! What would his wife say when he told her he had no money? She would stare at him and flush and say—'Didn't you go out every day to work?'— How would he tell her then so that she could understand quickly and spare him words?

"Morning came and the man ate his breakfast silently. There was no butter on the bread, and his wife seemed to be apologising to him for not having any. She said, 'We'll be able to start fair from to-morrow,' and when he snapped at her angrily she thought it was because he had to eat dry bread.

"He went to the park and sat there for hours. Now and again he got up and walked into a neighbouring street, but always, after half an hour or so, he came back. Six o'clock in the evening was his hour for going home. When six o'clock came he did not move, he still sat opposite the pond with his head bowed down into his arms. Seven o'clock passed. At nine o'clock a bell was rung and every one had to leave. He went also. He stood outside the gates looking on this side and on that. Which way would he go? All roads were alike to him, so he turned at last and walked somewhere. He did not go home that night. He never went home again. He never was heard of again anywhere in the wide world."

The voice ceased speaking and silence swung down again upon the little cell. The Philosopher had been listening intently to this story, and after a few minutes he spoke "When you go up this road there is a turn to the left and all the path along is bordered with trees—there are birds in the trees, Glory be to God! There is only one house on that road, and the woman in it gave us milk to drink. She has but one son, a good boy, and she said the other children were dead; she was speaking of a husband who went away and left her—'Why should he have been afraid to come home?' said she—'sure, I loved him.'"

After a little interval the voice spoke again "I don't know what became of the man I was speaking of. I am a thief, and I'm well known to the police everywhere. I don't think that man would get a welcome at the house up here, for why should he?"

Another, a different, querulous kind of voice came from the silence "If I knew a place where there was a welcome I'd go there as quickly as I could, but I don't know a place and I never will, for what good would a man of my age be to any person? I am a thief also. The first thing I stole was a hen out of a little yard. I roasted it in a ditch and ate it, and then I stole another one and ate it, and after that I stole everything I could lay my hands on. I suppose I will steal as long as I live, and I'll die in a ditch at the heel of the hunt. There was a time, not long ago, and if any one had told me then that I would rob, even for hunger, I'd have been insulted: but what does it matter now? And the reason I am a thief is because I got old without noticing it. Other people noticed it, but I did not. I suppose age comes on one so gradually that it is seldom observed. If there are wrinkles on one's face we do not remember when they were not there: we put down all kind of little infirmities to sedentary living, and you will see plenty of young people bald. If a man has no occasion to tell any one his age, and if he never thinks of it himself, he won't see ten years' difference between his youth and his age, for we live in slow, quiet times, and nothing ever happens to mark the years as they go by, one after the other, and all the same.

"I lodged in a house for a great many years, and a little girl grew up there, the daughter of my landlady. She used to slide down the bannisters very well, and she used to play the piano very badly. These two things worried me many a time. She used to bring me my meals in the morning and the evening, and often enough she'd stop to talk with me while I was eating. She was a very chatty girl and I was a talkative person myself. When she was about eighteen years of age I got so used to her that if her mother came with the food I would be worried for the rest of the day. Her face was as bright as a sunbeam, and her lazy, careless ways, big, free movements, and girlish chatter were pleasant to a man whose loneliness was only beginning to be apparent to him through her company. I've thought of it often since, and I suppose that's how it began. She used to listen to all my opinions and she'd agree with them because she had none of her own yet. She was a good girl, but lazy in her mind and body; childish, in fact. Her talk was as involved as her actions: she always seemed to be sliding down mental bannisters; she thought in kinks and spoke in spasms, hopped mentally from one subject to another without the slightest difficulty, and could use a lot of language in saying nothing at all. I could see all that at the time, but I suppose I was too pleased with my own sharp business brains, and sick enough, although I did not know it, of my sharp-brained, business companions—dear Lord! I remember them well. It's easy enough to have brains as they call it, but it is not so easy to have a little gaiety or carelessness or childishness or whatever it was she had. It is good, too, to feel superior to some one, even a girl.

"One day this thought came to me—'It is time that I settled down.' I don't know where the idea came from; one hears it often enough and it always seems to apply to some one else, but I don't know what brought it to roost with me. I was foolish, too: I bought ties and differently shaped collars, and took to creasing my trousers by folding them under the bed and lying on them all night—It never struck me that I was more than three times her age. I brought home sweets for her and she was delighted. She said she adored sweets, and she used to insist on my eating some of them with her; she liked to compare notes as to how they tasted while eating them. I used to get a toothache from them, but I bore with it although at that time I hated toothache almost as much as I hated sweets. Then I asked her to come out with me for a walk. She was willing enough and it was a novel experience for me. Indeed, it was rather exciting. We went out together often after that, and sometimes we'd meet people I knew, young men from my office or from other offices. I used to be shy when some of these people winked at me as they saluted. It was pleasant, too, telling the girl who they were, their business and their salaries: for there was little I didn't know. I used to tell her of my own position in the office and what the chief said to me through the day. Sometimes we talked of the things that had appeared in the evening papers. A murder perhaps, some phase of a divorce case, the speech a political person had made, or the price of stock. She was interested in anything so long as it was talk. And her own share in the conversation was good to hear. Every lady that passed us had a hat that stirred her to the top of rapture or the other pinnacle of disgust. She told me what ladies were frights and what were ducks. Under her scampering tongue I began to learn something of humanity, even though she saw most people as delightfully funny clowns or superb, majestical princes, but I noticed that she never said a bad word of a man, although many of the men she looked after were ordinary enough. Until I went walking with her I never knew what a shop window was. A jeweller's window especially: there were curious things in it. She told me how a tiara should be worn, and a pendant, and she explained the kind of studs I should wear myself; they were made of gold and had red stones in them; she showed me the ropes of pearl or diamonds that she thought would look pretty on herself: and one day she said that she liked me very much. I was pleased and excited that day, but I was a business man and I said very little in reply. I never liked a pig in a poke.

"She used to go out two nights in the week, Monday and Thursday, dressed in her best clothes. I didn't know where she went, and I didn't ask—I thought she visited an acquaintance, a girl friend or some such. The time went by and I made up my mind to ask her to marry me. I had watched her long enough and she was always kind and bright. I liked the way she smiled, and I liked her obedient, mannerly bearing. There was something else I liked, which I did not recognise then, something surrounding all her movements, a graciousness, a spaciousness: I did not analyse it; but I know now that it was her youth. I remember that when we were out together she walked slowly, but in the house she would leap up and down the stairs—she moved furiously, but I didn't.

"One evening she dressed to go out as usual, and she called at my door to know had I everything I wanted. I said I had something to tell her when she came home, something important. She promised to come in early to hear it, and I laughed at her and she laughed back and went sliding down the bannisters. I don't think I have had any reason to laugh since that night. A letter came for me after she had gone, and I knew by the shape and the handwriting that it was from the office. It puzzled me to think why I should be written to. I didn't like opening it somehow. . . It was my dismissal on account of advancing age, and it hoped for my future welfare politely enough. It was signed by the Senior. I didn't grip it at first, and then I thought it was a hoax. For a long time I sat in my room with an empty mind. I was watching my mind: there were immense distances in it that drowsed and buzzed; large, soft movements seemed to be made in my mind, and although I was looking at the letter in my hand I was really trying to focus those great, swinging spaces in my brain, and my ears were listening for a movement of some kind. I can see back to that time plainly. I went walking up and down the room. There was a dull, subterranean anger in me. I remember muttering once or twice, 'Shameful!' and again I said, 'Ridiculous!' At the idea of age I looked at my face in the glass, but I was looking at my mind, and it seemed to go grey, there was a heaviness there also. I seemed to be peering from beneath a weight at something strange. I had a feeling that I had let go a grip which I had held tightly for a long time, and I had a feeling that the letting go was a grave disaster. . . that strange face in the glass! how wrinkled it was! there were only a few hairs on the head and they were grey ones. There was a constant twitching of the lips and the eyes were deep-set, little and dull. I left the glass and sat down by the window, looking out. I saw nothing in the street: I just looked into a blackness. My mind was as blank as the night and as soundless. There was a swirl outside the window, rain tossed by the wind; without noticing, I saw it, and my brain swung with the rain until it heaved in circles, and then a feeling of faintness awakened me to myself. I did not allow my mind to think, but now and again a word swooped from immense distances through my brain, swinging like a comet across a sky and jarring terribly when it struck: 'Sacked' was one word, 'Old' was another word.

"I don't know how long I sat watching the flight of these dreadful words and listening to their clanking impact, but a movement in the street aroused me. Two people, the girl and a young, slender man, were coming slowly up to the house. The rain was falling heavily, but they did not seem to mind it. There was a big puddle of water close to the kerb, and the girl, stepping daintily as a cat, went round this, but the young man stood for a moment beyond it. He raised both arms, clenched his fists, swung them, and jumped over the puddle. Then he and the girl stood looking at the water, apparently measuring the jump. I could see them plainly by a street lamp. They were bidding each other good-bye. The girl put her hand to his neck and settled the collar of his coat, and while her hand rested on him the young man suddenly and violently flung his arms about her and hugged her; then they kissed and moved apart. The man walked to the rain puddle and stood there with his face turned back laughing at her, and then he jumped straight into the middle of the puddle and began to dance up and down in it, the muddy water splashing up to his knees. She ran over to him crying 'Stop, silly!' When she came into the house, I bolted my door and I gave no answer to her knock.

"In a few months the money I had saved was spent. I couldn't get any work, I was too old; they put it that they wanted a younger man. I couldn't pay my rent. I went out into the world again, like a baby, an old baby in a new world. I stole food, food, food anywhere and everywhere. At first I was always caught. Often I was sent to gaol; sometimes I was let go; sometimes I was kicked; but I learned to live like a wolf at last. I am not often caught now when I steal food. But there is something happening every day, whether it is going to gaol or planning how to steal a hen or a loaf of bread. I find that it is a good life, much better than the one I lived for nearly sixty years, and I have time to think over every sort of thing. . ."

When the morning came the Philosopher was taken on a car to the big City in order that he might be put on his trial and hanged. It was the custom.

BOOK 6

THE THIN WOMAN'S JOURNEY
AND THE HAPPY MARCH

Chapter 17

The ability of the Thin Woman of Inis Magrath for anger was unbounded. She was not one of those limited creatures who are swept clean by a gust of wrath and left placid and smiling after its passing. She could store her anger in those caverns of eternity which open into every soul, and which are filled with rage and violence until the time comes when they may be stored with wisdom and love; for, in the genesis of life, love is at the beginning and the end of things. First, like a laughing child, love came to labour minutely in the rocks and sands of the heart, opening the first of those roads which lead inwards for ever, and then, the labour of his day being done, love fled away and was forgotten. Following came the fierce winds of hate to work like giants and gnomes among the prodigious debris, quarrying the rocks and levelling the roads which soar inwards; but when that work is completed love will come radiantly again to live for ever in the human heart, which is Eternity.

Before the Thin Woman could undertake the redemption of her husband by wrath, it was necessary that she should be purified by the performance of that sacrifice which is called the Forgiveness of Enemies, and this she did by embracing the Leprecauns of the Gort and in the presence of the sun and the wind remitting their crime against her husband. Thus she became free to devote her malice against the State of Punishment, while forgiving the individuals who had but acted in obedience to the pressure of their infernal environment, which pressure is Sin.

This done she set about baking the three cakes against her journey to Angus Og.

While she was baking the cakes, the children, Seumas and Brigid Beg, slipped away into the wood to speak to each other and to wonder over this extraordinary occurrence.

At first their movements were very careful, for they could not be quite sure that the policemen had really gone away, or whether they were hiding in dark places waiting to pounce on them and carry them away to captivity. The word "murder" was almost unknown to them, and its strangeness was rendered still more strange by reason of the nearness of their father to the term. It was a terrible word and its terror was magnified by their father's unthinkable implication. What had he done? Almost all his actions and habits were so familiar to them as to be commonplace, and yet, there was a dark something to which he was a party and which dashed before them as terrible and ungraspable as a lightning-flash. They understood that it had something to do with that other father and mother whose bodies had been snatched from beneath the hearthstone, but they knew the Philosopher had done nothing in that instance, and, so, they saw murder as a terrible, occult affair which was quite beyond their mental horizons.

No one jumped out on them from behind the trees, so in a little time their confidence returned and they walked less carefully. When they reached the edge of the pine wood the brilliant sunshine invited them to go farther, and after a little hesitation they did so. The good spaces and the sweet air dissipated their melancholy thoughts, and very soon they were racing each other to this point and to that. Their wayward flights had carried them in the direction of Meehawl MacMurrachu's cottage, and here, breathlessly, they threw themselves under a small tree to rest. It was a thorn bush, and as they sat beneath it the cessation of movement gave them opportunity to again consider the terrible position of their father. With children thought cannot be separated from action for very long. They think as much with their hands as with their heads. They have to do the thing they speak of in order to visualise the idea, and, consequently, Seumas Beg was soon reconstructing the earlier visit of the policemen to their house in grand pantomime. The ground beneath the thorn bush became the hearthstone of their cottage; he and Brigid became four policemen, and in a moment he was digging furiously with a broad piece of wood to find the two hidden bodies. He had digged for only a few minutes when the piece of wood struck against something hard. A very little time sufficed to throw the soil off this, and their delight was great when they unearthed a beautiful little earthen crock filled to the brim with shining, yellow dust. When they lifted this they were astonished at its great weight. They played for a long time with it, letting the heavy, yellow shower slip through their fingers and watching it glisten in the sunshine. After they tired of this they decided to bring the crock home, but by the time they reached the Gort na Cloca Mora they were so tired that they could not carry it any farther, and they decided to leave it with their friends the Leprecauns. Seumas Beg gave the taps on the tree trunk which they had learned, and in a moment the Leprecaun whom they knew came up.

"We have brought this, sir," said Seumas. But he got no further, for the instant the Leprecaun saw the crock he threw his arms around it and wept in so loud a voice that his comrades swarmed up to see what had happened to him, and they added their laughter and tears to his, to which chorus the children subjoined their sympathetic clamour, so that a noise of great complexity rang through all the Gort.

But the Leprecauns' surrender to this happy passion was short. Hard on their gladness came remembrance and consternation; and then repentance, that dismal virtue, wailed in their ears and their hearts. How could they thank the children whose father and protector they had delivered to the unilluminated justice of humanity? that justice which demands not atonement but punishment; which is learned in the Book of Enmity but not in the Book of Friendship; which calls hatred Nature, and Love a conspiracy; whose law is an iron chain and whose mercy is debility and chagrin; the blind fiend who would impose his own blindness; that unfruitful loin which curses fertility; that stony heart which would petrify the generations of man; before whom life withers away appalled and death would shudder again to its tomb. Repentance! they wiped the inadequate ooze from their eyes and danced joyfully for spite. They could do no more, so they fed the children lovingly and carried them home.

The Thin Woman had baked three cakes. One of these she gave to each of the children and one she kept herself, whereupon they set out upon their journey to Angus Og.

It was well after midday when they started. The fresh gaiety of the morning was gone, and a tyrannous sun, whose majesty was almost insupportable, forded it over the world. There was but little shade for the travellers, and, after a time, they became hot and weary and thirsty—that is, the children did, but the Thin Woman, by reason of her thinness, was proof against every elemental rigour, except hunger, from which no creature is free.

She strode in the centre of the road, a very volcano of silence, thinking twenty different thoughts at the one moment, so that the urgency of her desire for utterance kept her terribly quiet; but against this crust of quietude there was accumulating a mass of speech which must at the last explode or petrify. From this congestion of thought there arose the first deep rumblings, precursors of uproar, and another moment would have heard the thunder of her varied malediction, but that Brigid Beg began to cry: for, indeed, the poor child was both tired and parched to distraction, and Seumas had no barrier against a similar surrender, but two minutes' worth of boyish pride. This discovery withdrew the Thin

Woman from her fiery contemplations, and in comforting the children she forgot her own hardships.

It became necessary to find water quickly: no difficult thing, for the Thin Woman, being a Natural, was like all other creatures able to sense the whereabouts of water, and so she at once led the children in a slightly different direction. In a few minutes they reached a well by the road-side, and here the children drank deeply and were comforted. There was a wide, leafy tree growing hard by the well, and in the shade of this tree they sat down and ate their cakes.

While they rested the Thin Woman advised the children on many important matters. She never addressed her discourse to both of them at once, but spoke first to Seumas on one subject and then to Brigid on another subject; for, as she said, the things which a boy must learn are not those which are necessary to a girl. It is particularly important that a man should understand how to circumvent women, for this and the capture of food forms the basis of masculine wisdom, and on this subject she spoke to Seumas. It is, however, equally urgent that a woman should be skilled to keep a man in his proper place, and to this thesis Brigid gave an undivided attention.

She taught that a man must hate all women before he is able to love a woman, but that he is at liberty, or rather he is under express command, to love all men because they are of his kind. Women also should love all other women as themselves, and they should hate all men but one man only, and him they should seek to turn into a woman, because women, by the order of their beings, must be either tyrants or slaves, and it is better they should be tyrants than slaves. She explained that between men and women there exists a state of unremitting warfare, and that the endeavour of each sex is to bring the other to subjection; but that women are possessed by a demon called Pity which severely handicaps their battle and perpetually gives victory to the male, who is thus constantly rescued on the very ridges of defeat. She said to Seumas that his fatal day would dawn when he loved a woman, because he would sacrifice his destiny to her caprice, and she begged him for love of her to beware of all that twisty sex. To Brigid she revealed that a woman's terrible day is upon her when she knows that a man loves her, for a man in love submits only to a woman, a partial, individual and temporary submission, but a woman who is loved surrenders more fully to the very god of love himself, and so she becomes a slave, and is not alone deprived of her personal liberty, but is even infected in her mental processes by this crafty obsession. The fates work for man, and therefore, she averred, woman must be victorious, for those who dare to war against the gods are already assured of victory: this being the law of life, that only the weak shall conquer. The limit of strength is petrifaction and immobility, but there is no limit to weakness, and cunning or fluidity is its counsellor. For these reasons, and in order that life might not cease, women should seek to turn their husbands into women; then they would be tyrants and their husbands would be slaves, and life would be renewed for a further period.

As the Thin Woman proceeded with this lesson it became at last so extremely complicated that she was brought to a stand by the knots, so she decided to resume their journey and disentangle her argument when the weather became cooler.

They were repacking the cakes in their wallets when they observed a stout, comely female coming towards the well. This woman, when she drew near, saluted the Thin Woman, and her the Thin Woman saluted again, whereupon the stranger sat down.

"It's hot weather, surely," said she, "and I'm thinking it's as much as a body's life is worth to be travelling this day and the sun the way it is. Did you come far, now, ma'am, or is it that you are used to going the roads and don't mind it?"

"Not far," said the Thin Woman.

"Far or near," said the stranger, "a perch is as much as I'd like to travel this time of the year. That's a fine pair of children you have with you now, ma'am."

"They are," said the Thin Woman.

"I've ten of them myself," the other continued, "and I often wondered where they came from. It's queer to think of one woman making ten new creatures and she not getting a penny for it, nor any thanks itself."

"It is," said the Thin Woman.

"Do you ever talk more than two words at the one time, ma'am?" said the stranger.

"I do," said the Thin Woman.

"I'd give a penny to hear you," replied the other angrily, "for a more bad-natured, cross-grained, cantankerous person than yourself I never met among womankind. It's what I said to a man only yesterday, that thin ones are bad ones, and there isn't any one could be thinner than you are yourself."

"The reason you say that," said the Thin Woman calmly, "is because you are fat and you have to tell lies to yourself to hide your misfortune, and let on that you like it. There is no one in the world could like to be fat, and there I leave you, ma'am. You can poke your finger in your own eye, but you may keep it out of mine if you please, and, so, good-bye to you; and if I wasn't a quiet woman I'd pull you by the hair of the head up a hill and down a hill for two hours, and now there's an end of it. I've given you more than two words; let you take care or I'll give you two more that will put blisters on your body for ever. Come along with me now, children, and if ever you see a woman like that woman you'll know that she eats until she can't stand, and drinks until she can't sit, and sleeps until she is stupid; and if that sort of person ever talks to you remember that two words are all that's due to her, and let them be short ones, for a woman like that would be a traitor and a thief, only that she's too lazy to be anything but a sot, God help her I and, so, good-bye."

Thereupon the Thin Woman and the children arose, and having saluted the stranger they went down the wide path; but the other woman stayed where she was sitting, and she did not say a word even to herself.

As she strode along the Thin Woman lapsed again to her anger, and became so distant in her aspect that the children could get no companionship from her; so, after a while, they ceased to consider her at all and addressed themselves to their play. They danced before and behind and around her. They ran and doubled, shouted and laughed and sang. Sometimes they pretended they were husband and wife, and then they plodded quietly side by side, making wise, occasional remarks on the weather, or the condition of their health, or the state of the fields of rye. Sometimes one was a horse and the other was a driver, and then they stamped along the road with loud, fierce snortings and louder and fiercer commands. At another moment one was a cow being driven with great difficulty to market by a driver whose temper had given way hours before; or they both became goats and with their heads jammed together they pushed and squealed viciously; and these changes lapsed into one another so easily that at no moment were they unoccupied. But as the day wore on to evening the immense surrounding quietude began to weigh heavily upon them. Saving for their own shrill voices there was no sound, and this unending, wide silence at last commanded them to a corresponding quietness. Little by little they ceased their play. The scamper became a trot, each run was more and more curtailed in its length, the race back became swifter than the run forth, and, shortly, they were pacing soberly enough one on either side of the Thin Woman sending back and forth a few quiet sentences. Soon even these sentences trailed away into the vast surrounding stillness. Then Brigid Beg clutched the Thin Woman's right hand, and not long after Seumas gently clasped her left hand, and these mute appeals for protection and comfort again released her from the valleys of fury through which she had been so fiercely careering.

As they went gently along they saw a cow lying in a field, and, seeing this animal, the Thin Woman stopped thoughtfully.

"Everything," said she, "belongs to the wayfarer," and she crossed into the field and milked the cow into a vessel which she had.

"I wonder," said Seumas, "who owns that cow."

"Maybe," said Brigid Beg, "nobody owns her at all."

"The cow owns herself," said the Thin Woman, "for nobody can own a thing that is alive. I am sure she gives her milk to us with great goodwill, for we are modest, temperate people without greed or pretension."

On being released the cow lay down again in the grass and resumed its interrupted cud. As the evening had grown chill the Thin Woman and the children huddled close to the warm animal. They drew pieces of cake from their wallets, and ate these and drank happily from the vessel of milk. Now and then the cow looked benignantly over its shoulder bidding them a welcome to its hospitable flanks. It had a mild, motherly eye, and it was very fond of children. The youngsters continually deserted their meal in order to put their arms about the cow's neck to thank and praise her for her goodness, and to draw each other's attention to various excellences in its appearance.

"Cow," said Brigid Beg in an ecstasy, "I love you."

"So do I," said Seumas. "Do you notice the kind of eyes it has?"

"Why does a cow have horns?" said Brigid.

So they asked the cow that question, but it only smiled and said nothing.

"If a cow talked to you," said Brigid, "what would it say?"

"Let us be cows," replied Seumas, "and then, maybe, we will find out."

So they became cows and ate a few blades of grass, but they found that when they were cows they did not want to say anything but "moo," and they decided that cows did not want to say anything more than that either, and they became interested in the reflection that, perhaps, nothing else was worth saying.

A long, thin, yellow-coloured fly was going in that direction on a journey, and he stopped to rest himself on the cow's nose.

"You are welcome," said the cow.

"It's a great night for travelling," said the fly, "but one gets tired alone. Have you seen any of my people about?"

"No," replied the cow, "no one but beetles to-night, and they seldom stop for a talk. You've rather a good kind of life, I suppose, flying about and enjoying yourself."

"We all have our troubles," said the fly in a melancholy voice, and he commenced to clean his right wing with his leg.

"Does any one ever lie against your back the way these people are lying against mine, or do they steal your milk?"

"There are too many spiders about," said the fly.

"No corner is safe from them; they squat in the grass and pounce on you. I've got a twist, my eye trying to watch them. They are ugly, voracious people without manners or neighbourliness, terrible, terrible creatures."

"I have seen them," said the cow, "but they never done me any harm. Move up a little bit please, I want to lick my nose: it's queer how itchy my nose gets"—the fly moved up a bit. "If," the cow continued, "you had stayed there, and if my tongue had hit you, I don't suppose you would ever have recovered."

"Your tongue couldn't have hit me," said the by. "I move very quickly you know."

Hereupon the cow slily whacked her tongue across her nose. She did not see the fly move, but it was hovering safely half an inch over her nose.

"You see," said the fly.

"I do," replied the cow, and she bellowed so sudden and furious a snort of laughter that the fly was blown far away by that gust and never came back again.

This amused the cow exceedingly, and she chuckled and sniggered to herself for a long time. The children had listened with great interest to the conversation, and they also laughed delightedly, and the Thin Woman admitted that the fly had got the worse of it; but, after a while, she said that the part of the cow's back against which she was resting was bonier than anything she had ever leaned upon before, and that while thinness was a virtue no one had any right to be thin in lumps, and that on this count the cow was not to be commended. On hearing this the cow arose, and without another look at them it walked away into the dusky field. The Thin Woman told the children afterwards that she was sorry she had said anything, but she was unable to bring her self to apologise to the cow, and so they were forced to resume their journey in order to keep themselves warm.

There was a sickle moon in the sky, a tender sword whose radiance stayed in its own high places and did not at all illumine the heavy world below; the glimmer of infrequent stars could also be seen with spacious, dark solitudes between them; but on the earth the darkness gathered in fold on fold of misty veiling, through which the trees uttered an earnest whisper, and the grasses lifted their little voices, and the wind crooned its thrilling, stern lament.

As the travellers walked on, their eyes, flinching from the darkness, rested joyfully on the gracious moon, but that joy lasted only for a little time. The Thin Woman spoke to them curiously about the moon, and, indeed, she might speak with assurance on that subject, for her ancestors had sported in the cold beam through countless dim generations.

"It is not known," said she, "that the fairies seldom dance for joy, but for sadness that they have been expelled from the sweet dawn, and therefore their midnight revels are only ceremonies to remind them of their happy state in the morning of the world before thoughtful curiosity and self-righteous moralities drove them from the kind face of the sun to the dark exile of midnight. It is strange that we may not be angry while looking on the moon. Indeed, no mere appetite or passion of any kind dare become imperative in the presence of the Shining One; and this, in a more limited degree, is true also of every form of beauty; for there is something in an absolute beauty to chide away the desires of materiality and yet to dissolve the spirit in ecstasies of fear and sadness. Beauty has no liking for Thought, but will send terror and sorrow on those who look upon her with intelligent eyes. We may neither be angry nor gay in the presence of the moon, nor may we dare to think in her bailiwick, or the Jealous One will surely afflict us. I think that she is not benevolent but malign, and that her mildness is a cloak for many shy infamies. I think that beauty tends to become frightful as it becomes perfect, and that, if we could see it comprehendingly, the extreme of beauty is a desolating hideousness, and that the name of ultimate, absolute beauty is Madness. Therefore men should seek loveliness rather than beauty, and so they would always have a friend to go beside them, to understand and to comfort them, for that is the business of loveliness: but the business of beauty—there is no person at all knows what that is. Beauty is the extreme which has not yet swung to and become merged in its opposite. The poets have sung of this beauty and the philosophers have prophesied of it, thinking that the beauty which passes all understanding is also the peace which passeth understanding; but I think that whatever passes understanding, which is imagination, is terrible, standing aloof from humanity and from kindness, and that this is the sin against the Holy Ghost, the great Artist. An isolated perfection is a symbol of terror and pride, and it is followed only by the head of man, but the heart winces from it aghast, cleaving to that loveliness which is modesty and righteousness. Every extreme is bad, in order that it may swing to and fertilize its equally horrible opposite."

Thus, speaking more to herself than to the children, the Thin Woman beguiled the way. The moon had brightened as she spoke, and on either side of the path, wherever there was a tree or a rise in the ground, a black shadow was crouching tensely watchful, seeming as if it might spring into terrible life at a bound. Of these shadows the children became so fearful that the Thin Woman forsook the path and adventured on the open hillside, so that in a short time the road was left behind and around them stretched the quiet slopes in the full shining of the moon.

When they had walked for a long time the children became sleepy; they were unused to being awake in the night, and as there was no place where they could rest, and as it was evident that they could not walk much further, the Thin Woman grew anxious. Already Brigid had made a tiny, whimpering sound, and Seumas had followed this with a sigh, the slightest prolongation of which might have trailed into a sob, and when children are overtaken by tears they do not understand how to escape from them until they are simply bored by much weeping.

When they topped a slight incline they saw a light shining some distance away, and toward this the Thin Woman hurried. As they drew near she saw it was a small fire, and around this some figures were seated. In a few minutes she came into the circle of the firelight, and here she halted suddenly. She would have turned and fled, but fear loosened her knees so that they would not obey her will; also the people by the fire had observed her, and a great voice commanded that she should draw near.

The fire was made of branches of heather, and beside it three figures sat. The Thin Woman, hiding her perturbation as well as she could, came nigh and sat down by the fire. After a low word of greeting she gave some of her cake to the children, drew them close to her, wrapped her shawl about their heads and bade them sleep. Then, shrinkingly, she looked at her hosts.

They were quite naked, and each of them gazed on her with intent earnestness. The first was so beautiful that the eye failed upon him, flinching aside as from a great brightness. He was of mighty stature, and yet so nobly proportioned, so exquisitely slender and graceful, that no idea of gravity or bulk went with his height. His face was kingly and youthful and of a terrifying serenity. The second man was of equal height, but broad to wonderment. So broad was he that his great height seemed diminished. The tense arm on which he leaned was knotted and ridged with muscle, and his hand gripped deeply into the ground. His face seemed as though it had been hammered from hard rock, a massive, blunt face as rigid as his arm. The third man can scarcely be described. He was neither short nor tall. He was muscled as heavily as the second man. As he sat he looked like a colossal toad squatting with his arms about his knees, and upon these his chin rested. He had no shape nor swiftness, and his head was flattened down and was scarcely wider than his neck. He had a protruding dog-like mouth that twitched occasionally, and from his little eyes there glinted a horrible intelligence. Before this man the soul of the Thin Woman grovelled. She felt herself crawling to him. The last terrible abasement of which humanity is capable came upon her: a fascination which would have drawn her to him in screaming adoration. Hardly could she look away from him, but her arms were about the children, and love, mightiest of the powers, stirred fiercely in her heart.

The first man spoke to her.

"Woman," said he, "for what purpose do you go abroad on this night and on this hill?"

"I travel, sir," said the Thin Woman, "searching for the Brugh of Angus the son of the Dagda Mor."

"We are all children of the Great Father," said he. "Do you know who we are?"

"I do not know that," said she.

"We are the Three Absolutes, the Three Redeemers, the three Alembics—the Most Beautiful Man, the Strongest Man and the Ugliest Man. In the midst of every strife we go unhurt. We count the slain and the victors and pass on laughing, and to us in the eternal order come all the peoples of the world to be regenerated for ever. Why have you called to us?"

"I did not call to you, indeed," said the Thin Woman; "but why do you sit in the path so that travellers to the House of the Dagda are halted on their journey?"

"There are no paths closed to us," he replied; "even the gods seek us, for they grow weary in their splendid desolation—saving Him who liveth in all things and in us; Him we serve and before His awful front we abase ourselves. You, O Woman, who are walking in the valleys of anger, have called to us in your heart, therefore we are waiting for you on the side of the hill. Choose now one of us to be your mate, and do not fear to choose, for our kingdoms are equal and our powers are equal."

"Why would I choose one of you," replied the Thin Woman, "when I am well married already to the best man in the world?"

"Beyond us there is no best man," said he, "for we are the best in beauty, and the best in strength, and the best in ugliness; there is no excellence which is not contained in us three. If you are married what does that matter to us who are free from the pettiness of jealousy and fear, being at one with ourselves and with every manifestation of nature."

"If," she replied, "you are the Absolute and are above all pettiness, can you not be superior to me also and let me pass quietly on my road to the Dagda!"

"We are what all humanity desire," quoth he, "and we desire all humanity. There is nothing, small or great, disdained by our immortal appetites. It is not lawful, even for the Absolute, to outgrow Desire, which is the breath of God quick in his creatures and not to be bounded or surmounted by any perfection."

During this conversation the other great figures had leaned forward listening intently but saying nothing. The Thin Woman could feel the children like little, terrified birds pressing closely and very quietly to her sides.

"Sir," said she, "tell me what is Beauty and what is Strength and what is Ugliness? for, although I can see these things, I do not know what they are."

"I will tell you that," he replied—"Beauty is Thought and Strength is Love and Ugliness is Generation. The home of Beauty is the head of man. The home of Strength is the heart of man, and in the loins Ugliness keeps his dreadful state. If you come with me you shall know all delight. You shall live unharmed in the flame of the spirit, and nothing that is gross shall bind your limbs or hinder your thought. You shall move as a queen amongst all raging passions without torment or despair. Never shall you be driven or ashamed, but always you will choose your own paths and walk with me in freedom and contentment and beauty."

"All things," said the Thin Woman, "must act according to the order of their being, and so I say to Thought, if you hold me against my will presently I will bind you against your will, for the holder of an unwilling mate becomes the guardian and the slave of his captive."

"That is true," said he, "and against a thing that is true I cannot contend; therefore, you are free from me, but from my brethren you are not free."

The Thin Woman turned to the second man.

"You are Strength?" said she.

"I am Strength and Love," he boomed, "and with me there is safety and peace; my days have honour and my nights quietness. There is no evil thing walks near my lands, nor is any sound heard but the lowing of my cattle, the songs of my birds and the laughter of my happy children. Come then to me who gives protection and happiness and peace, and does not fail or grow weary at any time."

"I will not go with you," said the Thin Woman, "for I am a mother and my strength cannot be increased; I am a mother and my love cannot be added to. What have I further to desire from thee, thou great man?"

"You are free of me," said the second man, "but from my brother you are not free."

Then to the third man the Thin Woman addressed herself in terror, for to that hideous one something cringed within her in an ecstasy of loathing. That repulsion which at its strongest becomes attraction gripped her. A shiver, a plunge, and she had gone, but the hands of the children withheld her while in woe she abased herself before him.

He spoke, and his voice came clogged and painful as though it urged from the matted pores of the earth itself.

"There is none left to whom you may go but me only. Do not be afraid, but come to me and I will give you these wild delights which have been long forgotten. All things which are crude and riotous, all that is gross and without limit is mine. You shall not think and suffer any longer; but you shall feel so surely that the heat of the sun will be happiness: the taste of food, the wind that blows upon you, the ripe ease of your body—these things will amaze you who have forgotten them. My great arms about you will make you furious and young again; you shall leap on the hillside like a young goat and sing for joy as the birds sing. Leave this crabbed humanity that is barred and chained away from joy and come with me, to whose ancient quietude at the last both Strength and Beauty will come like children tired in the evening, returning to the freedom of the brutes and the birds, with bodies sufficient for their pleasure and with no care for Thought or foolish curiosity."

But the Thin Woman drew back from his hand, saying "It is not lawful to turn again when the journey is commenced, but to go forward to whatever is appointed; nor may we return to your meadows and trees and sunny places who have once departed from them. The torments of the mind may not be renounced for any easement of the body until the smoke that blinds us is blown away, and the tormenting flame has fitted us for that immortal ecstasy which is the bosom of God. Nor is it lawful that ye great ones should beset the path of travellers, seeking to lure them away with cunning promises. It is only at the cross-roads ye may sit where the traveller will hesitate and be in doubt, but on the highway ye have no power."

"You are free of me," said the third man, "until you are ready to come to me again, for I only of all things am steadfast and patient, and to me all return in their seasons. There are brightnesses in my secret places in the woods, and lamps in my gardens beneath the hills, tended by the angels of God, and behind my face there is another face not hated by the Bright Ones."

So the three Absolutes arose and strode mightily away; and as they went their thunderous speech to each other boomed against the clouds and the earth like a gusty wind, and, even when they had disappeared, that great rumble could be heard dying gently away in the moonlit distances.

The Thin Woman and the children went slowly forward on the rugged, sloping way. Far beyond, near the distant summit of the hill there was a light gleaming.

"Yonder," said the Thin Woman, "is the Brugh of Angus Mac an Og, the son of the Dagda Mor," and toward this light she assisted the weary children.

In a little she was in the presence of the god and by him refreshed and comforted. She told him all that had happened to her husband and implored his assistance. This was readily accorded, for the chief business of the gods is to give protection and assistance to such of their people as require it; but (and this is their limitation) they cannot give any help until it is demanded, the freewill of mankind being the most jealously guarded and holy principle in life; therefore, the interference of the loving gods comes only on an equally loving summons.

Chapter 18

Caitilin Ni Murrachu sat alone in the Brugh of Angus much as she had sat on the hillside and in the cave of Pan, and again she was thinking. She was happy now. There was nothing more she could desire, for all that the earth contained or the mind could describe was hers. Her thoughts were no longer those shy, subterranean gropings which elude the hand and the understanding. Each thought was a thing or a person, visible in its own radiant personal life, and to be seen or felt, welcomed or repulsed, as was its due. But she had discovered that happiness is not laughter or satisfaction, and that no person can be happy for themselves alone. So she had come to understand the terrible sadness of the gods, and why Angus wept in secret; for often in the night she had heard him weeping, and she knew that his tears were for those others who were unhappy, and that he could not be comforted while there was a woeful person or an evil deed hiding in the world. Her own happiness also had become infected with this alien misery, until she knew that nothing was alien to her, and that in truth all persons and all things were her brothers and sisters and that they were living and dying in distress; and at the last she knew that there was not any man but mankind, nor any human being but only humanity. Never again could the gratification of a desire give her pleasure for her sense of oneness was destroyed—she was not an individual only; she was also part of a mighty organism ordained, through whatever stress, to achieve its oneness, and this great being was threefold, comprising in its mighty units God and Man and Nature—the immortal trinity. The duty of life is the sacrifice of self: it is to renounce the little ego that the mighty ego may be freed; and, knowing this, she found at last that she knew Happiness, that divine discontent which cannot rest nor be at ease until its bourne is attained and the knowledge of a man is added to the gaiety of a child. Angus had told her that beyond this there lay the great ecstasy which is Love and God and the beginning and the end of all things; for everything must come from the Liberty into the Bondage, that it may return again to the Liberty comprehending all things and fitted for that fiery enjoyment. This cannot be until there are no more fools living, for until the last fool has grown wise wisdom will totter and freedom will still be invisible. Growth is not by years but by multitudes, and until there is a common eye no one person can see God, for the eye of all nature will scarcely be great enough to look upon that majesty. We shall greet Happiness by multitudes, but we can only greet Him by starry systems and a universal love.

She was so thinking when Angus Og came to her from the fields. The god was very radiant, smiling like the young morn when the buds awake, and to his lips song came instead of speech.

"My beloved," said he, "we will go on a journey today."

"My delight is where you go," said Caitilin.

"We will go down to the world of men—from our quiet dwelling among the hills to the noisy city and the multitude of people. This will be our first journey, but on a time not distant we will go to them again, and we will not return from that journey, for we will live among our people and be at peace."

"May the day come soon," said she.

"When thy son is a man he will go before us on that journey," said Angus, and Caitilin shivered with a great delight, knowing that a son would be born to her.

Then Angus Og put upon his bride glorious raiment, and they went out to the sunlight. It was the early morning, the sun had just risen and the dew was sparkling on the heather and the grass. There was a keen stir in the air that stung the blood to joy, so that Caitilin danced in uncontrollable gaiety, and Angus, with a merry voice, chanted to the sky and danced also. About his shining head the birds were flying; for every kiss he gave to Caitilin became a bird, the messengers of love and wisdom, and they also burst into triumphant melody, so that the quiet place rang with their glee. Constantly from the circling birds one would go flying with great speed to all quarters of space. These were his messengers flying to every fort and dun, every rath and glen and valley of Eire to raise the Sluaige Shee (the Fairy Host). They were birds of love that flew, for this was a hosting of happiness, and, therefore the Shee would not bring weapons with them.

It was towards Kilmasheogue their happy steps were directed, and soon they came to the mountain.

After the Thin Woman of Inis Magrath had left the god she visited all the fairy forts of Kilmasheogue, and directed the Shee who lived there to be in waiting at the dawn on the summit of the mountain; consequently, when Angus and Caitilin came up the hill, they found the six clans coming to receive them, and with these were the people of the younger Shee, members of the Tuatha da Danaan, tall and beautiful men and women who had descended to the quiet underworld when the pressure of the sons of Milith forced them with their kind enchantments and invincible velour to the country of the gods.

Of those who came were Aine Ni Rogail of Cnoc Aine and Ivil of Craglea, the queens of North and South Munster, and Una the queen of Ormond; these, with their hosts, sang upon the summit of the hill welcoming the god. There came the five guardians of Ulster, the fomentors of combat:—Brier Mac Belgan of Dromona Breg, Redg Rotbill from the slopes of Magh-Itar, Tinnel the son of Boclacthna of Slieve Edlicon, Grici of Cruachan-Aigle, a goodly name, and Gulban Glas Mac Grici, whose dun is in the Ben of Gulban. These five, matchless in combat, marched up the hill with their tribes, shouting as they went. From north and south they came, and from east and west, bright and happy beings, a multitude, without fear, without distraction, so that soon the hill was gay with their voices and their noble raiment.

Among them came the people of the Lupra, the ancient Leprecauns of the world, leaping like goats among the knees of the heroes. They were headed by their king Udan Mac Audain and Beg Mac Beg his tanist, and, following behind, was Glomhar O'Glomrach of the sea, the strongest man of their people, dressed in the skin of a weasel; and there were also the chief men of that clan, well known of old, Conan Mac Rihid, Gaerku Mac Gairid, Mether Mac Mintan and Esirt Mac Beg, the son of Bueyen, born in a victory. This king was that same Udan the chief of the Lupra who had been placed under bonds to taste the porridge in the great cauldron of Emania, into which pot he fell, and was taken captive with his wife, and held for five weary years, until he surrendered that which he most valued in the world, even his boots: the people of the hills laugh still at the story, and the Leprecauns may still be mortified by it.

There came Bove Derg, the Fiery, seldom seen, and his harper the son of Trogain, whose music heals the sick and makes the sad heart merry; Rochy Mac Elathan, Dagda Mor, the Father of Stars, and his daughter from the Cave of Cruachan; Credh Mac Aedh of Raghery and Cas Corach son of the great Ollav; Mananaan Mac Lir came from his wide waters shouting louder than the wind, with his daughters Cliona and Aoife and Etain Fair-Hair; and Coll and Cecht and Mac Greina, the Plough, the Hazel, and the Sun came with their wives, whose names are not forgotten, even Banba and Fodla and Eire, names of glory. Lugh of the Long-Hand, filled with mysterious wisdom, was not absent, whose father was sadly avenged on the sons of Turann—these with their hosts.

And one came also to whom the hosts shouted with mighty love, even the Serene One, Dana, the Mother of the gods, steadfast for ever. Her breath is on the morning, her smile is summer. From her hand the birds of the air take their food. The mild ox is her friend, and the wolf trots by her friendly side; at her voice the daisy peeps from her cave and the nettle couches his lance. The rose arrays herself in innocence, scattering abroad her sweetness with the dew, and the oak tree laughs to her in the air. Thou beautiful! the lambs follow thy footsteps, they crop thy bounty in the meadows and are not thwarted: the weary men cling to thy bosom everlasting. Through thee all actions and the deeds of men, through thee all voices come to us, even the Divine Promise and the breath of the Almighty from afar laden with goodness.

With wonder, with delight, the daughter of Murrachu watched the hosting of the Shee. Sometimes her eyes were dazzled as a jewelled forehead blazed in the sun, or a shoulder-torque of broad gold flamed like a torch. On fair hair and dark the sun gleamed: white arms tossed and glanced a moment and sank and reappeared. The eyes of those who did not hesitate nor compute looked into her eyes, not appraising, not questioning, but mild and unafraid. The voices of free people spoke in her ears and the laughter of happy hearts, unthoughtful of sin or shame, released from the hard bondage of selfhood. For these people, though many, were one. Each spoke to the other as to himself, without reservation or subterfuge. They moved freely each in his personal whim, and they moved also with the unity of one being: for when they shouted to the Mother of the gods they shouted with one voice, and they bowed to her as one man bows. Through the many minds there went also one mind, correcting, commanding, so that in a moment the interchangeable and fluid became locked, and organic with a simultaneous understanding, a collective action—which was freedom.

While she looked the dancing ceased, and they turned their faces with one accord down the mountain. Those in the front leaped forward, and behind them the others went leaping in orderly progression.

Then Angus Og ran to where she stood, his bride of Beauty "Come, my beloved," said he, and hand in hand they raced among the others, laughing as they ran.

Here there was no green thing growing; a carpet of brown turf spread to the edge of sight on the sloping plain and away to where another mountain soared in the air. They came to this and descended. In the distance, groves of trees could be seen, and, very far away, the roofs and towers and spires of the Town of the Ford of Hurdles, and the little roads that wandered everywhere; but on this height there was only prickly furze growing softly in the sunlight; the bee droned his loud song, the birds flew and sang occasionally, and the little streams grew heavy with their falling waters. A little further and the bushes were green and beautiful, waving their gentle leaves in the quietude, and beyond again, wrapped in sunshine and peace, the trees looked on the world from their calm heights, having no complaint to make of anything.

In a little they reached the grass land and the dance began. Hand sought for hand, feet moved companionably as though they loved each other; quietly intimate they tripped without faltering, and, then, the loud song arose—they sang to the lovers of gaiety and peace, long defrauded "Come to us, ye who do not know where ye are—ye who live among strangers in the house of dismay and self-righteousness. Poor, awkward ones! How bewildered and bedevilled ye go! Amazed ye look and do not comprehend, for your eyes are set upon a star and your feet move in the blessed kingdoms of the Shee Innocents! in what prisons are ye flung? To what lowliness are ye bowed? How are ye ground between the laws and the customs? The dark people of the Fomor have ye in thrall; and upon your minds they have fastened a band of lead, your hearts are hung with iron, and about your loins a cincture of brass impressed, woeful! Believe it, that the sun does shine, the flowers grow, and the birds sing pleasantly in the trees. The free winds are everywhere, the water tumbles on the hills, the eagle calls aloud through the solitude, and his mate comes speedily. The bees are gathering honey in the sunlight, the midges dance together, and the great bull bellows across the river. The crow says a word to his brethren, and the wren snuggles her young in the hedge. . . Come to us, ye lovers of life and happiness. Hold out thy hand—a brother shall seize it from afar. Leave the plough and the cart for a little time: put aside the needle and the awl—Is leather thy brother, O man? . . . Come away! come away! from the loom and the desk, from the shop where the carcasses are hung, from the place where raiment is sold and the place where it is sewn in darkness: O bad treachery! Is it for joy you sit in the broker's den, thou pale man? Has the attorney enchanted thee? . . . Come away! for the dance has begun lightly, the wind is sounding over the hill, the sun laughs down into the valley, and the sea leaps upon the shingle, panting for joy, dancing, dancing, dancing for joy. . ."

They swept through the goat tracks and the little boreens and the curving roads. Down to the city they went dancing and singing; among the streets and the shops telling their sunny tale; not heeding the malignant eyes and the cold brows as the sons of Balor looked sidewards. And they took the Philosopher from his prison, even the Intellect of Man they took from the hands of the doctors and lawyers, from the sly priests, from the professors whose mouths are gorged with sawdust, and the merchants who sell blades of grass—the awful people of the Fomor. . . and then they returned again, dancing and singing, to the country of the gods. . .

A Note About the Author

James Stephens (1880–1950) was a Dublin-born writer whose work was a celebration of Irish identity. As a poet and novelist, he produced original stories and vibrant retellings of classic myths. His most notable titles include *The Charwoman's Daughter*, *The Crock of Gold*, and *The Insurrection in Dublin*, a bold account of 1916's Easter Rebellion. Stephen's working-class roots and national pride made him a fixture during the Irish Literary Revival alongside peers W.B. Yeats and Padraic Colum.

A Note from the Publisher

Spanning many genres, from non-fiction essays to literature classics to children's books and lyric poetry, Mint Edition books showcase the master works of our time in a modern new package. The text is freshly typeset, is clean and easy to read, and features a new note about the author in each volume. Many books also include exclusive new introductory material. Every book boasts a striking new cover, which makes it as appropriate for collecting as it is for gift giving. Mint Edition books are only printed when a reader orders them, so natural resources are not wasted. We're proud that our books are never manufactured in excess and exist only in the exact quantity they need to be read and enjoyed.

bookfinity™

Discover more of your favorite classics with Bookfinity™.

- Track your reading with custom book lists.
- Get great book recommendations for your personalized Reader Type.
- Add reviews for your favorite books.
- AND MUCH MORE!

Visit **bookfinity.com** and take the fun Reader Type quiz to get started.

Enjoy our classic and modern companion pairings!

Printed in the USA
CPSIA information can be obtained
at www.ICGtesting.com
JSHW021416160824
R13664500001B/R136645PG68134JSX00013B/25

9 781513 266688